"Blood," she said softly.

"The blood of the genetically pure, Balzan. This is what the seven stones must have, this is what they must bathe in, if they are to give off their life-providing rays. The blood of a sentient being, a strong, intelligent being. The sort of man who would survive the Games despite all odds. A man such as you," she finished.

Balzan shivered. He was locked in a palace chamber with the mysterious queen. He was hearing secrets no one had learned before—and stayed alive!

THE
BLOOD STONES

Wallace Moore

PYRAMID BOOKS  NEW YORK

THE BLOOD STONES
A PYRAMID BOOK

Produced by Lyle Kenyon Engel

Copyright © 1975 by Lyle Kenyon Engel

Pyramid edition published May 1975

ISBN 0-515-03628-5

Library of Congress Catalog Card Number: 75-4463

Printed in the United States of America

───────────────────────────────────

Pyramid Books are published by Pyramid Communications, Inc. Its trademarks, consisting of the word "Pyramid" and the portrayal of a pyramid, are registered in the United States Patent Office.

Pyramid Communications, Inc., 919 Third Avenue, New York, N.Y. 10022

THE
BLOOD STONES

Chapter One

The zanth stalked through the forest, a shadow among shadows, its low scaly head swinging from side to side, its red eyes peering into the yellow foliage bordering the path. It growled softly as it moved, a rumble working its way up from deep within its leathery chest and escaping from between the twin ridges of bone which served the zanth for teeth. It was hunting; it sensed its prey; drawing back its gray lips, the zanth snarled and moved into a moonlit clearing, pausing for several seconds to scent the air.

Something was here. Something was watching . . . something alien and strange.

Nervously, the zanth padded around the perimeter of the clearing, studying the darkness at the far side of the grassy area. Overhead the twin moons moved more closely together in their nightly passage, filling the clearing with a cool white light almost as bright as day. The zanth's eyes flickered, became hooded; a nocturnal creature, the zanth wasn't accustomed to strong light. It stared at the shadows near a large tree; that was where the scent came from, somewhere near the trunk. The alien-thing was there, watching the zanth and waiting to attack. Again the zanth's lips drew back, exposing the cutting edge of its teeth. Its muscles tensed, rippled, bunched—and with a snarl, the zanth leaped.

A figure darted from the cover of the tree, avoiding the zanth's lunge. Landing, the zanth whirled and attacked anew, this time missing only by a matter of inches, its jaws clacking together just above the alien-thing's thigh.

7

The zanth drew back, hissing and snarling, glaring at the creature crouching before it. The scent was *wrong;* this creature didn't belong in the zanth's forest, it wasn't part of the zanth's world. It was different, strange: its body was too long, its limbs too thin and lanky, not like the limbs of the other bipeds the zanth had seen and attacked in recent days—no, not like those bipeds at all. It wore the dress of those creatures, the hide covering on chest and legs, the pads on its feet; it even carried the weapon of those creatures—the short blade, glistening in the moonlight. But its skin was a pale color, not bright yellow, and it had no tail, and no claws on its paws. Its eyes were blue and its head was covered with dark hair, longer than any fur the zanth had ever seen. Most of all, it was bald; except for the hair on its crown, the creature was completely naked. It reeked of *alien*ness; it was frighteningly unknown. Confused and afraid, the zanth hissed and shook itself, and once again, lunged.

Somehow the figure managed to duck under the zanth's leap. The zanth felt a sudden sharp pain along its belly as the alien's knife sliced its stomach open, there was a brief burst of crimson fire, and then—darkness.

The zanth never realized it had died.

Balzan saw the zanth before the beast saw him. He'd been stalking the zanth for almost an hour, staying to the trees above the forest path, dropping behind whenever he felt he was getting too close, or when the wind changed and threatened to carry his scent. The zanth hadn't seen him, or had pretended not to. It'd been an interesting hunt, a game he'd played before with other, less dangerous prey, but the time had come to bring it to a close. Swinging ahead of the beast, catching a limb of the tree before him an instant after he dove, repeating this until he reached a clearing that was large enough for a confrontation, Balzan reviewed the hunt procedure in his mind and decided he was ready. There could be no further delay; the time had arrived.

He'd never fought a zanth before, and he knew of only a few members of his tribe who had and had lived. Of all the beasts in the North Forest, the zanth was easily the most deadly. Eight feet long, covered with a thick and almost impenetrable hide, its neck protected by a ridge of bone, the zanth had been responsible for a number of deaths among the Cat People in recent weeks. To please Lomar and Kitta, Balzan had avoided the zanth until this moment; after the previous night's killing, he could do so no longer. The girl who'd been slain—her body slashed and torn, unrecognizable when she was found—had been the daughter of Balzan's teacher, Dhurn. It'd been obvious what he had to do, regardless of Lomar's wishes. That it *was* obvious was the reason why he was here.

Reaching the upper limb of a thick-trunked tree at the far edge of the clearing, Balzan waited until he saw the zanth leave the protection of the foliage before he moved. He dropped to the ground beside the tree and took his hunting knife from its sheath on his belt beside Balzan's therb. The knife fit his hand snugly; it was a larger knife than those used by others of the Cat People tribe. Balzan was taller than the average Endorian, broader across the shoulders, a husky young man in his early twenties. His face was sharp-featured, unlike the somewhat blurred feline features of his fellows; he was beardless; his shaggy hair was thick across his head, cropped close to his shoulders, and held away from his eyes by a leather band. He was different from the Endorians in other ways as well: his hands had five fingers as opposed to their four, and his voice, when he spoke, was richer and deeper than the Endorian norm. He was of a different race; it was apparent to his "brothers," if not to him.

He stood within the shadow of the vast tree and watched the zanth leave the cover at the clearing's far end and come toward him. "Now," he whispered softly. "Now." He tensed, then forced himself to relax. When the attack came, he'd be ready—or he wouldn't. It would have to be a matter of reflex; there wasn't any way he could prepare himself to anticipate—

The zanth leaped, shrieking.

For an instant Balzan thought he wouldn't move quickly enough, that he was dead, a breathing corpse. Then he was diving, hitting the grass and rolling, coming back on his feet before he could finish the thought. He felt the zanth sail past him, its hide brushing his arm as they passed each other. Without thinking, he turned. The zanth threw itself at him, howling and snapping its jaws. Just barely, he sidestepped the rush. His heart was jerking in his chest, pulsing behind his temples. Coming around, he realized the zanth was lunging for the kill, jumping high to tear into his throat and rip his head off. He stumbled back and almost fell, paralyzed.

The zanth's eyes seemed to fill his vision; he stared at them in an almost hypnotic state. Reflexively, he dropped to his knee as the beast kicked off. Again reflexively, he shoved the hunting knife up and caught the zanth in the belly as it passed over him. The blade sank deep. The zanth's momentum carried it over Balzan's shoulder and tumbled it into the grass and bushes at the end of the clearing, rolling it several times through the dirt. It was dead when it stopped moving.

Balzan stood up on shaking legs and looked down at the knife in his hand. It was sticky with green blood, gore smeared over it and his hand and arm, some of it spattered on his chest and shoulder. After a moment he looked at the zanth, where it lay crumpled and twisted in the dirt, its limbs splayed out, blind eyes staring at the double moons in the sky overhead. Tension drained out of him, flooding from him like blood from a deep wound. He closed his eyes and brushed his clean hand over his forehead and face; opening his eyes, he blinked at the blood now wetting his palm.

Finally he bent over and was sick.

2.

He heard the scream as he was kneeling to skin the dead zanth. Pausing, he stopped with his knife inserted partially under the heavy hide and glanced up. The scream came again almost immediately, shrill and long, breaking over the sounds of the forest and drowning the calls of the birds and insects; it rose suddenly and cut off. He waited, but there were no more cries, only silence. Complete silence: even the forest sounds were gone. . . .

He tilted his head and listened intently, eyes closed.

It *might* have been his imagination. The village was almost a mile away, in a valley below the level of the forest where he'd met the zanth. Still, perhaps he *could* hear the sound of metal striking metal and steel thudding into flesh; he couldn't really be certain, but there might have been shouts, commands, the snorting of gaapurs—

There were. He was sure of it now. The Endorian village was under attack; probably by the Albs, the eternal enemies of the Cat People. A mile away, his friends and brothers were fighting for their lives while he knelt beside the decaying corpse of an animal, knife in hand, helpless to aid them. The muscles of his shoulders knotted; his hand tensed; he cried out and jumped to his feet, plunging the knife into its sheath. Without another look at the zanth, he left the clearing, breaking into a run when he came to the path he'd followed an hour before. Head low, he ran, ignoring the branches which whipped against his skin, shutting out the swelling pound of blood through his chest and face. He ran like a blind man, oblivious to everything around him, aware only of the sounds which became clearer as he neared the village, the shouts and panicked cries of death.

There were at least a hundred Albs in the village, all of them armed and half of them mounted. Balzan broke out of the forest into the field north of the village and halted, breathing in short, ragged gasps. He could see that it was a massacre; there was blood everywhere, half a dozen huts were burning, and the Albs were riding through the lanes like emerald-skinned demons—it was a nightmare. As he caught his breath, Balzan saw one of the Albs on horseback—a dark reptilian with a long, bony snout, wearing a commander's vest and armor—point at him and shout something to a foot soldier nearby. The Alb soldier answered his commander and turned to face Balzan across

11

the field, drawing his sword. "Oh, god," Balzan said angrily. *"Damn* it! Damn it to hell!"

Stepping forward to approach the foot soldier, Balzan unhooked his therb from its place on his belt and shook it out to its full length. Forty feet of whip, tipped with a sharp barb, the therb was an ingenious and deadly weapon: its handle contained poison, which was fed through the length to its tip, where it was discharged each time the barb struck flesh. Balzan walked toward the Alb wearily. "You're a fool," he said, "a damn fool. Do you hear me? A *fool.*"

Seeing the therb, the foot soldier leered. His lizard-face broke open and exposed a gaping red mouth and a ridge of sharp bone. He hissed and waved his sword, which cut a strange, glistening arc, shining in the moonlight. The Alb commander, watching from the saddle of his gaapur, nodded approvingly, spat out something else to the foot soldier and wheeling his mount around, galloped back into the village proper. Balzan stopped walking thirty feet away from the Alb soldier; he stood waiting. After several seconds of hissing and waving his sword, the Alb grinned—in a way—and started forward.

The therb cracked; the Alb staggered back and put a hand to his shoulder, where the barb had snapped against armor. Balzan watched. The Alb shifted his heavy balancing tail uneasily as he examined the small dent in the armor, then peered at Balzan with wary yellow eyes. He was about average height for a member of his reptilian race; his body was about a head shorter than Balzan's, heavily scaled, short and squat, equipped with legs like tree stumps and a weighty tail that was almost as long as the Alb was tall. He wore armor on his chest and groin, yet otherwise went naked; his scales provided all the climate protection he ever would need. "I told you," Balzan said. "You're a fool."

Less sure of himself now, the Alb started toward the young man again, this time hefting his shield and holding it to protect his flat-featured face. Yellow eyes moved nervously in the green face; a red tongue flicked between lipless jaws. Balzan shook his head and sighed.

"You think you're brave?" Balzan asked quietly. He swung the therb up and cracked it down with a flick of his wrist. The barbed tip shot out and licked the Alb's forehead over the reptilian brow. "You're not brave, you're stupid." The Alb's eyes widened—seemingly an impossible feat, since he had no eyelids—his lizard jaw dropped, clapped shut, gaped again; for a moment he seemed about to scream. Balzan flicked the therb once more. The barb snapped into the Alb's right eye. With a shriek of pain and horror, the soldier twisted around, dropped his sword and shield and fell heavily to the ground. "Stupid," Balzan said, nearing the still-twitching corpse. "Not brave."

The body jerked one final time and was still. "You've seen the therb before," the young man said, standing over the motionless soldier. "You couldn't have believed you could beat me. . . ."

A sound caught his attention, and Balzan looked up. Near him a hut was burning, crackling as its wooden walls crumpled into ash and collapsed as he watched. He recognized the charred plaque over the doorway before it fell. It had been Dhurn's hut, whose daughter had been killed by the zanth, whose hut had been a second home to Balzan when he was a child. Dhurn was the oldest of the Endorians, and he'd treated the young Balzan well, not commenting on the differences between Lomar's adopted son and the other children, apparently not noticing the lack of fur, the absent tail, the heavy and unwieldy limbs. Dhurn had been kind to him, as kind as Lomar and his stepsister, Kitta. When Balzan saw that it was the old Endorian's hut which was crumbling into cinders, something broke within his mind. He screamed and charged forward, his thoughts lost in rage.

Ahead of him, in the village, Balzan could see the Albs moving back and forth, entering huts and carrying out screaming women, knocking men to the ground, trampling the Endorians too old or too young to get out of the soldiers' way. The stench of smoke was bitter around Balzan as he ran, the stink of burning wood and the acrid odor of charred flesh making him cough and choke. He stumbled over a body lying in the road and looked down. It was Chato, a woman he'd known as long as he'd known Dhurn. Her face was a broken, bloody mask. The feline lines were crushed and ruined, the fur matted with some pulpy material. She was still breathing when he found her, but as he bent to touch her, her mouth bubbled blood and her eyes went dead. Fires rose within him. He staggered away from Chato's body, no longer aware of the carnage around him and no longer seeing the blood or hearing the screams. His mind went blank; he stumbled and ran.

At last, he saw them. Six Albs, a hundred yards away, crowding around their gaapurs, throwing several unconscious Endorians over the saddles like sacks of grain. They were laughing and talking among themselves. Balzan saw them and cried out; like a zanth sensing blood, he charged.

The one nearest the street saw Balzan first. Hissing, the Alb dropped the reins of his gaapur—a maned animal as tall as the Alb's shoulder, domesticated and used as a mount—and spun to meet Balzan's rush. The young man's leap carried him into the Alb's chest, hard. His head struck the armor, stunning him; both of them fell to the ground and rolled in the muddy road, each struggling to get the upper hand. Laughing, the Alb's friends backed away to give them room, forming a half circle around the fighters. One of the soldiers was about to make a wager concerning the outcome, when the Alb on top of Balzan stiffened suddenly and dropped onto the ground, a knife hilt protruding from the soft, unscaled skin of his armpit.

Balzan rolled to his feet while the remaining Albs were still gaping at their dead comrade. He grabbed the blade from the fallen soldier's sheath and swung it in an arc that sliced through two of the standing Albs and connected fleetingly with a third. He was expecting to feel the sword rebound from the first Alb's armor; instead, the blade cleaved the soldier neatly, slashing through his armor, and the armor of the Alb next to him, and the armor of the third.

All three Albs were dead in an instant, their entrails spilling from the gaping wounds appearing across their stomachs and chests.

"What?" Balzan stared at the blade in his fist. Its edge glistened and seemed to waver as he looked at it. The sword caught the moonlight and shattered it into a thousand stars along its length, flickering brightly. "What—?" he started to say again; he didn't get a chance to finish the sentence . . . the two living Albs jumped at him as soon as their fellows fell to the ground.

Twisting and bringing his sword up, Balzan parried the first Alb's blow, meeting the edge of the soldier's blade with his own. Steel sparked against steel; lightning scattered away from the contact. Balzan drew back, caught the lunge of the Alb on his right, slipped his sword under the guard of the lead Alb and cut his blade upward through the Alb's armor and chest. It was as though he were slicing through grease; the sword moved without resistance, gutting the Alb lengthwise like a fish. Before the gutted soldier fell, Balzan had turned and decapitated the other; the two Albs slumped to the ground together, a bloody heap of green blood, scales and split armor.

"What *is* this?" He held the sword at arm's length and studied it in awe. Now he understood why the foot soldier had attacked him so boldly; with a weapon like this, a man couldn't help but feel invincible. But where had it come from? The Albs weren't capable of designing a sword like the one he held; it was impossible . . . .

Yet there it was, gleaming in his hand like a length of solid lightning.

Several moments passed before he shivered, broke his attention away from the blade, and looked around. He was at the intersection of two lanes, just a few dozen yards from the hut he shared with Lomar and Kitta. Orienting himself in the smoke, he trotted downhill. He realized that the shouts and cries behind him were fading; he made out the sound of gaapur hooves on muddy earth, receding. Biting his lip, he increased his speed and arrived at Lomar's tent-hut in time to see a band of seven or eight Albs take off around the hut, toward the west. There was no question about following the riders; the scene outside the doorway of the hut claimed Balzan completely.

Lomar was on his stomach, bleeding from an ugly

15

wound on his shoulder, a tear in the fur and flesh that ran from his neck to the upper part of his arm. The old Endorian's face was twisted in a grimace of pain, the ordinarily handsome features blurred by a veil of blood. Balzan shifted his gaze and saw the Alb coming through the doorway: it was the field commander, a giant of a soldier, Balzan's height at least, wearing armor under his command vest, on his arms and legs as well as his chest. The Alb caught sight of Balzan moments after the young man saw him. Roaring, the Alb commander drew a sword similar to the one Balzan held, and swinging the blade over his head like a banner, plunged toward the startled young man before Balzan could move.

Sword met sword, sparking. Balzan wasn't used to the weight of the blade; it seemed to change as he fought, becoming heavier or lighter, depending on the angle in which he used it. Twice Balzan almost found the Alb's blade sticking between his ribs. Each time he avoided the commander's thrust and answered it with one of his own. The Alb smacked his jaws, showing Balzan the dark red interior of his mouth; he was enjoying the battle, in fact he was *playing* with Balzan, using his tricks to make the young man sweat. Suddenly understanding this, Balzan disengaged his sword and drew back. The Alb laughed and followed him, cutting his blade through the air, causing it to glisten in the pale light of the twin moons.

Ducking behind a hut, Balzan dropped the strange blade and pulled out his therb. He was ready for the Alb when the commander rounded the corner, sneering and shouting. The Alb's features registered shock and surprise the instant before he dropped to the ground, the small cut on his scaly cheek showing where the poison barb had connected—no other mark on him, only the mark of death.

3.

"Easy. Don't move. I'll have to bandage that before I'll let you turn over."

"What good can a strip of cloth do? I can tell, Balzan; the wound is serious. I'm finished."

"Quiet. I'll be back in a moment."

He went into the hut and rummaged through a basket of clothing near the door. Most of the outfits were strewn about the room, together with the bed mats, the decorating sashes, Lomar's drinking bowls, Kitta's loom and Balzan's quiver of arrows; the bow was lying half under a mat in the corner, broken into three sections. Balzan glanced at it and shook his head, his mouth pressed into a grim line. Finally he found what he was looking for among the remaining clean clothes, a strip of cloth used as a ceremonial sash during feasts. He brought it outside and knelt beside Lomar, and used it to wrap the old Endorian's shoulder, pulling the sash snug and tying it under Lomar's arm. A moment later the cloth was soaked with blood.

"Are they gone?" the old man asked him.

"I haven't heard anything for several minutes. I think so. Don't worry about it; just rest, close your eyes. . . ."

Lomar peered at Balzan; his four-fingered hand came up and wiped some of the blood from the side of his head, clearing his vision. Lomar's fur was almost white, and in places it was matted; still, he was not really an old man, not in terms of Endorian society. As Balzan knew, there was still a great deal of fire in Lomar . . . but as the young man watched, he could see that fire going out.

"How did it happen?" Balzan asked. Lomar seemed to start, as though he'd been on the verge of sleeping.

"It's been weeks since they attacked," Lomar said. "Weeks. We thought they'd migrated. It would have been so easy if they'd simply gone away. . . ."

Balzan sighed, resting back on his haunches. "It's never that easy, Lomar. You should know that by now. We've been through this before." He touched the old man's good shoulder tenderly. "I was hunting the zanth; that's why I wasn't here when they attacked. Can you tell me how they managed to get into the village? We've beaten the Albs back before."

"I told you not to . . ."

"That's not the point," Balzan said. "How did the Albs break past our defenses?"

"They had weapons," Lomar said weakly. His eyes shut, but he continued to speak, though only in a half-whisper. Balzan bent closer to hear. "Swords we'd never seen before, and the way they used them . . . cut us down like a harvest crop. . . ."

"You mean they all had blades like that?"

"All."

Balzan leaned back, stunned. He could imagine how it'd been: the Endorians facing the Albs, outnumbering them forty to one, and yet completely unable to cope with those vicious swords. No wonder it had been a massacre. It couldn't have been anything else.

"I'm sorry, Lomar," he said softly.

The old Cat-man's eyes opened, the olive slits stared at him, curious. "You? And why are you sorry, Balzan?"

"Because I wasn't here when you needed me. It's my fault you're injured." *Dying*.

"Nonsense. We all have to take care of ourselves, Balzan. That's the nature of things. You were doing the thing you thought was necessary for you to do; it's simply a misfortune you weren't here, nothing more. Perhaps even good fortune; you might be lying here yourself."

Balzan started to reply, but couldn't. He opened his mouth, shut it, and looked around. There were bodies in the road nearby, and some of them were female, but none of them looked like—

"Kitta," he said abruptly. "Where is she?"

Lomar opened his eyes, which he'd closed again. "Gone," he said.

Balzan felt something tingle at his spine, cold and dry. "What do you mean? Where is she, Lomar?"

"Your sister is gone, Balzan," the old man said slowly. "Your sister and my daughter, is gone."

"She's dead?"

"She might as well be dead," Lomar replied.

At first Balzan didn't comprehend the old man's meaning; then it came to him, and he straightened, a red flush of rage and shame coloring his face. "They took her? The Albs?"

"She isn't your concern now, Balzan," the old Endorian said urgently. He pushed himself into a half-sitting position with his good arm. "Fight while fighting is feasible; surrender when the fight is lost. The dead are dead; you can't bring them back through revenge. Kitta is one of the dead now, as far as you are concerned. She's gone. She's dead."

"To you, perhaps."

"It can be no other way, Balzan. Kitta is *dead*."

The young man swung to his feet. "Even if she were, I'd still have to go after them. You have to know that, Lomar. It's the way I am."

"Just as you went after the zanth?"

"Just as I went after the zanth," Balzan answered.

Lomar sighed, a low whistle through half-closed lips. "You *are* different," he said. He parted his lips to say something further; nothing came out. Balzan looked away.

The old man was dead.

4.

It was one of many funerals that day, but for Balzan it was the single most dramatic event of his life. The flames licking around Lomar's shroud-covered form seemed to consume more than the dead man's flesh; Balzan felt as though the flames were consuming part of him too, a part of his soul. He remained by the pyre until dawn, keeping vigil with the other mourners, but he left before any of them, before the ashes were cold. Stopping at the hut he'd lived in with Lomar and Kitta for twenty-odd years, he retrieved his arrows and quiver, and the gut for the bow, had sheathed the Alb sword in a makeshift sheath on his belt and had turned to leave the small room when Dhurn appeared in the doorway. The ancient's bent form was framed in the light of the dawning sun, a silhouette limned in red and gold.

"You're leaving?"

19

Balzan shrugged. "I don't have any choice."

"You have many choices," Dhurn said. His voice quavered. Balzan could remember a time when the Endorian's tone was pleasant and demanding; now it seemed unsure and miserable. "Why have you chosen death?"

"It doesn't have to be death," Balzan said.

Dhurn lifted his hands and dropped them against the sides of his robe in despair. "Do what you will." He stepped aside to allow Balzan to move past him into the brightening light. The village looked mean and barren. Its remaining huts were deserted, painfully empty and alone. People wandered aimlessly through the streets, occasionally stopping to huddle in on themselves, or to bend and salvage something from the road. Dhurn noticed Balzan's expression and said, "In a few days they'll forget. One has to forget, Balzan."

"Does one, Dhurn?" Balzan looked at the older man, at the lines almost hidden under his facial fur, at the emptiness reflected in the ancient yellow eyes. "I wonder."

Slipping his quiver over his shoulder, Balzan stared down the path toward the south. Dhurn followed behind him for half a dozen paces, then stopped and watched the young man walk on.

"Will you come back?" he called.

"I don't know," Balzan answered, over his shoulder.

"Do you go to face them now?"

Balzan halted at the edge of the village and gazed back. Dhurn stood a hundred yards away, a diminutive figure in the crimson light of the morning sun. "Not now," Balzan said. He had to shout. "I've other things to do first. Important things."

Before the old Endorian could ask what things, Balzan strode the remaining distance to the forest, found an opening in the foliage and was gone from view.

Chapter Two

Three miles south of the Endorian village the forest gave way to a plain—broken here and there by a lonely yrrl tree—which stretched to the far horizon and touched the distant blue-gray hills. Balzan came to the plain an hour after dawn, before the morning light had burned off the dew and mist. Hurrying through the knee-high grass, he ran at an easy pace, angling southwest toward an outcropping of trees and boulders. One very large boulder dominated the copse, an immense gray weight covered completely by a scarlet vine. Reaching the copse, Balzan dropped to his stomach on the ground near the vine-shrouded object—revealed now to be made of metal, not stone—and pressed a section of the "boulder" with his right hand.

A section of the boulder lifted, displaying a dark area beyond. Sliding up, the metal section glinted sharply in the dawn light, reflecting Balzan's tense features in those places where the vine didn't reach. The young man pushed himself forward, grabbed the edges of the opening and drew himself inside. The section of rock slid home behind him.

Balzan's feet touched a cool metal surface. Around him, the darkness was shattered by light as two dozen floodlights blinked on in the ceiling. He was in a room twelve feet across by fifteen feet, a chamber crowded with pieces of electronic equipment of varying degrees of complexity and size. The room was painfully low, and Balzan was forced to crouch as he crossed the chamber, weaving between tubular constructs and rectangular machines, reaching a console that covered the entire wall. There was a chair slung low before the console under a large opaque screen. Balzan dropped into the chair with an audible sigh of relief and stretched out his full length, closing his eyes against the harsh cold light. He remained relaxed for several seconds, breathing deeply, forcing himself to ease the tensions from his body. He'd learned from long experience that the Teacher didn't react well to a tense operator.

By the time he'd calmed himself, Balzan was aware that the chamber was totally activated. Somewhere something hummed; a light was flashing on and off again patiently on the console; the huge screen glowed softly in anticipation of his first question, and the chair in which he reclined had finished adjusting itself to his figure. All that remained was for Balzan to place his hand on the QUERY plate, a flat rectangle on the chair's right arm, above a row of toggles and buttons. He did so. The screen brightened and formed an image in large block letters.

QUERY MEDIA: VERBAL/VISUAL

"Verbal," Balzan said quietly. He remembered with amusement his confusion the first time the screen had flickered on; it'd been a confusion mixed with terror and curiosity, and though the confusion had passed, and the terror had been muted by understanding, the curiosity had remained. Balzan suspected it would always remain.

"YES?" said the computer.

"There was a raid on the village," Balzan said. "Lomar was killed, my stepsister Kitta was kidnapped, and half the villagers were slain."

"AND THE ATTACKERS?"

"The Albs."

"SUBSPECIES OF REPTILIAN ORIGIN, CULTURE LEVEL D4, GEOGRAPHICAL LOCATION 74 DEGREES LONGITUDE, 43 DEGREES 12 MINUTES LATITUDE. PHYSICAL DESCRIPTION—"

"I know what they look like," Balzan said. He ran his hand over the arm of the chair, touching the buttons and depressions whose purpose he'd never divined. "That

22

isn't what concerns me. They have a new kind of weapon, a sword. I've brought one along for you to analyze."

"PLACE IT ON THE SENSOR PLATE."

Balzan got out of the chair and withdrew the sword from its makeshift sheath, placing it on a grid below the screen. Light flooded up through the grid, bathing the sword in green. Balzan returned to his chair and watched, pursing his lips and idly fingering the buttons near the QUERY plate. The light pulsed under the sword, abruptly flashed out; Balzan turned his head to avoid the glare.

"REPORT: ITEM IS FORTY-FIVE-POINT-SEVEN-TY-TWO CENTIMETERS IN LENGTH, WEIGHS ONE-POINT-SIX-EIGHT KILOGRAMS, PRIMARILY OPAQUE TO VISUAL SPECTRUM RADIATION. COMPOSITION: ION-CHARGED METAL, ATOMIC NUMBER TWENTY-SIX, ATOMIC WEIGHT FIFTY-FIVE-POINT-EIGHT-FIVE, ELEMENT NAME: IRON. ITEM IS CHARGED NEGATIVELY, A NEUTRON SHIELD APPROXIMATELY POINT-THREE-SEVEN MILIMETERS IN DEPTH COATING ONE EDGE OF THE ITEM. ITEM HAS AN ORNATE BASE, DECORA-TED WITH—"

"Cancel," Balzan said impatiently. "What do you mean, coated with a neutron shield?"

"VARIATION OF STANDARD PROTECTIVE SHIELD, A FORCE EFFECT POTENTIAL FIRST THEORIZED IN NINETEEN HUNDRED NINETY-FOUR ANNO DOMINI BY—"

"Cancel." Balzan leaned forward eagerly. "If I under-stand you correctly, this 'neutron shield' can act as a cut-ting edge?"

"AFFIRMATIVE." The screen flashed from a light blue to a soft white, as though showing approval of Balzan's question.

"Could the Albs have come up with something like this on their own?"

"NEGATIVE. CULTURE MATRIX INDICATES A LOW ORDER OF TECHNOLOGY. ITEM IS PROD-UCT OF A CULTURE AT LEVEL M2, AT THE LEAST."

"I see."

23

Relaxing in his chair, Balzan forced himself to unwind. His hands tapped a tattoo on the arm of the chair, as, frowning, he closed his eyes and reviewed what he'd learned from the Teacher in the past twenty years of his conscious life.

It was just possible he'd found a way to return home.

2.

There had been no computer error, the Teacher had assured him, nor had there been a human error. What had happened had been an accident, no more—a freak occurrence that wouldn't be duplicated in a million, or twice a million years. Almost defensively, the computer had reviewed the incident for him a thousand times, each time pointing out how the ship hadn't been at fault, and though he'd never seriously questioned the computer's explanation, Balzan accepted the story with reservation, not because he couldn't believe it, but because it seemed such a foolish way for a brilliant man and his wife to die. . . .

The year two thousand five hundred on Earth: that was when it'd begun.

For many years, mankind had been trying to forget the past, to wipe out the faulty judgment which had nearly destroyed the planet, the unthinking carelessness which had polluted the atmosphere and murdered the ocean; these failings were part of a different race, a more immature race, and as such they had to be buried and forgotten, so that mankind—the new, wiser mankind—could look to the future, and a bold new world.

In a way the prophets of doom could never have predicted in the mid-twentieth century, technology had triumphed on Earth. True, there were no more free forests, no more unpolluted water—but there *were* some good things about twenty-sixth-century Earth: there was a way of life which fulfilled a man completely, a life style that presented constant challenge and self-exploration. In the year 2500, a man could expect to spend almost half his lifetime educating himself to the wonders around him. It was an unending process, this education, a constant explosion of learning and ideas. For some men it was an orgasm of discovery; but for Professor Weldon Rice of the Technic Institute, it was a nightmare of unrealized dreams.

Rice was a scientist, an extraterrestrial biologist, interested in exploring the infinite variety of life in space. He was a brilliant man, a leader in his field, and in the thirty-odd years of his life he'd made more than his share of contributions to science. But at the same time he was a simple man, unable to cope with the pace of modern life and unwilling to compromise his view of the proper existence for an individual man. His wife Katherine agreed with his views. She was also a scientist, trained in nuclear engineering and highly regarded among her peers, but she was dissatisfied with the way things seemed to slip from her grasp. Experiences, knowledge, ethics, even memories —nothing seemed permanent, nothing existed simply to be enjoyed. Critics in the 1970s had called America the disposable society; in the year 2500, their mocking condemnation had taken on a new, more terrible meaning. It *was* a disposable society, a society in constant flux, moving and shifting, changing with frightening speed. And as far as Weldon Rice and his wife were concerned, the speed was *too* frightening. They wanted to get out, and when the opportunity presented itself, they did.

The project's official name was ARES PROBE ONE, but to the fifteen men and women directly involved with the planning and administration of the mission, it was SPACE FLIGHT: WAR-GOD. Both Weldon and Katherine were connected with the project, and were aware of the dangers the flight presented; still, when approached by the project directors to man the ARES PROBE space vessel on its flight and planned landing on Mars, Rice and his wife immediately agreed. They were to establish a base on Mars, the first manned base to be erected by humans on the red planet, and they accepted the mission for two reasons: first, because they saw it as a way of escaping a world which had become increasingly intolerable, and second, because Katherine Rice was pregnant with their first child.

The prospect of a child growing to adulthood on Mars was exciting to the project's planners, and they arranged to fill the space ship with extra teaching equipment, in the form of an eighth-generation analog computer, to aid the Rices in the child's upbringing. Paul Brian Rice was born in New Zealand at the project's main base, two months before the scheduled launching of ARES PROBE ONE; he was placed in a specially designed safety cube for protection during the trip, where he would rest in stasis until ARES PROBE settled on the dusty surface of the fourth planet. Everything was readied; Weldon and Katherine Rice said farewell to the world of their birth; and on a cool autumn evening in 2500, the red and gold exhaust of ARES ONE's shuttle rocket painted the New Zealand sky orange, lasting for only a few seconds until the shuttle passed from view on its way to the main ship orbiting above; six hours later, the spacecraft began its fourteen-month journey.

In the thirteenth month, something happened.

Here the computer was vague and contradictory, as though it doubted the evidence of its "senses," and was hesitant to report what it couldn't confirm. Apparently all had gone well for the first year of the voyage: Rice and his wife had spent the time completing their preparations for establishing the Mars Base, since the spacecraft required little from them by way of piloting. There'd been moments of boredom, but these had passed. As the hour of arrival drew nearer, Weldon and Katherine became more and more excited, spending more time each day at the view screens, studying the still-small globe of Mars until their eyes burned from the strain.

Weldon Rice was at the viewscreen when *it* occurred.

The Teacher reported Weldon's shriek, and the delayed shriek of Katherine Rice; it detailed the sudden acceleration the space ship underwent; it showed Balzan the visual recording made at the time, the revealing blur of white light mingled with emerald; but it could offer no explanation why ARES PROBE ONE suddenly *blanked out* completely; it couldn't explain what had happened in those ten seconds during which the computer itself had been

26

"unconscious"; the Teacher could only tell Balzan what it "saw" when its sensors began working once more.

What it saw was a totally alien sun and a rapidly approaching planet, and two moons spinning over a world which didn't exist in the solar system.

What it saw was a nightmare, for the spacecraft ARES PROBE ONE was no longer *in* the solar system, or, for that matter, within a hundred thousand light-years of the star called Sol. Somehow the spaceship had been *transferred*, plucked from its solar orbit and whooshed through space, and set down here, over a planet unlike any seen before by man.

A space warp? Those were only words, phrase making; a space warp didn't *mean* anything, it was a null statement, it equated to zero. But it was the only rational possibility for what had happened: the ARES PROBE had passed through a warp in the fabric of space, and instead of landing on the familiar red sentinel of the evening sky on Earth, the Rices' spacecraft was about to crash on an unknown and possibly hostile world.

Their *craft*, not them. Both Weldon Rice and Katherine had died in the instant of transferral. Only Paul Brian Rice survived, sleeping in stasis within his safety cube, unaware of the tragedy occurring around him. Blissfully ignorant—for the moment at least.

The ship had crashed; in time, an inhabitant of the world—the Endorian named Lomar, then a young biped vaguely resembling an earth cat—found the craft where it had crashed on a lonely plain. Lomar had discovered the long-dead bodies, and soon after came across the safety cube. Upon his touch, the cube opened, revealing the sleeping Paul Rice. Out of compassion, Lomar had adopted the orphan and had buried his parents; he brought the child back to the village and presented him to his natural daughter, Kitta, whose mother had died during childbirth. He named the earth-child Balzan, after a hero of the Cat People, and taught the child all he knew of the ways of the world. As the years passed, Balzan grew and learned of the sky-ship, and eventually visited the vine-covered remains of the spaceship, and slowly, painfully, learned the story of his origin . . . and the story of his parents' death.

Now he sat in the chair he'd sat in so many times before, and wondered . . . could the technology which produced a neutron sword also build a spacecraft?

And did that mean he could return to the world of his birth, the world he'd never seen—the legendary planet of men called Earth?

It was a question he put to the computer, not quite certain if he were willing to hear the answer.

3.

"THE POSSIBILITY IS PRESENT," the Teacher said. "A CULTURE CAPABLE OF PRODUCING A FORCE POTENTIAL EFFECT COULD ALSO THEORETICALLY CREATE THE TECHNOLOGY NECESSARY FOR—"

"Cancel," Balzan said. "I see what you mean." He got out of the chair and retrieved the neutron-sword, and was placing it in its sheath when another thought struck him. Leaning over the arm of the chair, he pressed his fingers down on the QUERY plate and craned his neck around to look up at the screen. "Teacher, there are times when I can't understand the people of my tribe, when they act oddly, the way they feel is completely alien to me. . . ."

"DIFFERENT CULTURAL MATRICES PRODUCE DIFFERING INDIVIDUALS."

"That's too simple an answer. I grew up in Endore; the Cat People are my people, my brothers. Why am I different?"

"A PORTION OF YOUR CULTURAL BACKGROUND WAS DEVELOPED HERE, DURING THOSE PERIODS IN WHICH YOU WERE PRESENTED WITH KNOWLEDGE BEYOND THAT PROVIDED BY YOUR NORMAL MATRIX."

There was a smug tone to the computer's cold mechanical voice; at least it seemed that way to Balzan. He smiled and was about to lift his hand from the plate, but stopped, frowning; a question had come to him, one he'd asked a thousand times and for which he'd never received a satisfactory answer. He asked it again, not certain what he expected to hear.

"Teacher," he said, "You've told me I am a man, and you've said a great many things about 'cultural matrices,' and 'background civilization,' and so on. But what *is* a man, Teacher? What makes him different from Lomar, or Kitta, or an Alb?"

"MAN: SPECIES OF PRIMATE EVOLVED ON SOL TWO DURING EARLY MESO—"

"Cancel."

With a sigh, he removed his hand from the chair arm and swung away from the console. It didn't really matter; the answer had little or no bearing on his future that he could see. For the present he was going to be too involved with the Albs, seeking out Kitta and the other kidnapped Endorians, and finding revenge for their deaths, if such was needed, to be concerned with questions of identity. He knew his name and he knew his capabilities. Everything else was irrelevant.

It was midday when he clambered out of the half-buried spacecraft. The sun was a circle of fire overhead, a bloody red in the pale gray sky. If he had any luck at all, he'd reach the Alb encampment before twilight; if he had no luck at all, it would hardly make a difference when he arrived. He pressed his lips into a tight line, remembering the death of Lomar, the burning of Dhurn's hut, the blackened corpse that had once been Chato. He had reason enough to seek out the Albs, even if they didn't lead him to a workable spacecraft. At the moment, he burned to see an Alb's green blood. . . .

Touching the hilt of his new sword, assuring himself that it was there and he hadn't forgotten it, he struck off across the field, pushing southwest through the knee-high grass. He didn't glance back at the ruined spaceship; in a way, he knew he would never see it again.

As he walked, he whistled. It wasn't a pleasant tune.

Chapter Three

Keno left the lower level of the barracks and climbed the short stairway to the surface, weaving only slightly as he lifted the tent flap and stepped up into the deepening twilight. The guard lying beside the flap blinked at Keno groggily, recognized him and held up a half-full flask of sarn. Keno waved it aside.

"I've had my fill," he told the guard. "Going for a walk around the camp perimeter."

The guard shrugged his scaly shoulders and shut his eyes. Keno stepped over the Alb's outstretched legs and tail and staggered through the darkness of the camp toward the distant trees. He stumbled once over a drunken soldier sprawled among the shattered remains of some empty flasks, one outstretched arm draped over the immobile form of a strangled Endorian wench. Seeing the dead girl reminded Keno of the Cat-woman he'd taken several hours earlier, after the raid on the Endorian village, and the memory made him smile. She'd struggled at first, but after a while she'd become complacent enough, even receptive. It was the nature of the beast, Keno reflected; they loved to fight, but they loved surrender more. Thinking that, he laughed. Laughing, he came to the edge of the camp, where the fire-cast shadows joined the trees of the North Wood. It was quiet here; peaceful.

Keno liked the quiet, though the peacefulness made him nervous. He found himself a spot near a cluster of boulders and sank to the ground with a sigh. He was drunk, too drunk; he'd be sick in the morning and depressed the entire day, but for now he felt warm and protected.

Closing his eyes, he listened to the whispering forest sounds, the chatter of insects, the mellow call of one night-bird to another, the sounds he'd lived with all his life; he was resting there, half-aware of the night surrounding him, when he heard a sound which was out of place among the noises of the forest—the crunch of approaching footsteps.

He was about to call out and ask if it was his friend, Yurn, but a hand clamped across his mouth and a knife pressed into the folds of his tunic. He opened his eyes and found himself staring at a demon torn from his worst nightmares.

"I'm glad I caught you alone," the demon said. Its face was a naked pink, its eyes blue, its skin neither furred nor scaled. "We're going to have a talk, you and I." The demon's knife dug into Keno's side, penetrating the cloth of the tunic. "And make no mistake: either we talk, or you die."

Despite the hand holding his mouth, Keno managed a frantic nod.

"Good," the demon said, smiling and displaying a gleaming set of teeth. "Let's start."

Balzan watched the Alb soldier with disgust; he'd followed the Alb's progress across the camp to the trees and it was apparent the soldier was drunk, almost unconscious on his feet—not at all the sort of subject for the questions Balzan wanted answered. Still, this was the first Alb to venture close enough to the forest to suit Balzan's purpose, and after waiting a full hour, he felt he was justified in being a bit disappointed. As he watched, Balzan saw the Alb stagger to a halt a few yards away and lower himself to the ground beside a clump of boulders; when he was sure no one else was near enough to hear them, Balzan dropped from his vantage point in a yrrl tree and padded through the grass to the soldier's side. The Alb reacted pretty much as Balzan expected. After taking several moments to impress the Alb with his sincerity, Balzan removed his hand from the creature's snout and leaned back on his haunches, waiting.

"What do you want to know?" The Alb's voice was heavy and grating, and though he and Balzan spoke the same language, the Alb's dialect differed considerably from the version of the language Balzan was accustomed to. He had the Alb repeat himself, then asked:

"The prisoners you took from the Endorian village: where are they?"

The Alb answered calmly. "Gone. They've left."

Calmly, Balzan pressed the point of the knife into the Alb's middle just below the creature's chest. The tip of the blade slipped between two scales, evoking a grunt of pain from the soldier and a reflexive snap of his jaws. "It's the truth," the Alb said as Balzan jerked the blade-tip free. "They were taken away hours ago."

Judging by the look in the Alb's eyes as he stared at the blade in the young man's hand, Balzan decided the creature wasn't lying. Balzan's suspicions were correct. "Taken by whom? And where—where were they taken?"

"By the Kharnites, of course."

"Why 'of course'? Who are these 'Kharnites'?"

The Alb grinned, exposing its bloody mouth and glistening ridges of bone. "They're the masters of us all, or so they say. They'll learn differently when we've finished with them. You'll see. The Albs *have* no masters."

"You haven't told me who they are."

"They came to us two dozen nights ago, when the moons were in their dark face. They showed us wonders: swords we'd never seen before, sky-boats drawn by gaapurs, armor which could reflect any arrow . . ." Despite his earlier bravado, the Alb's voice took on a tone of awe. "They promised to give us these things if we delivered a quota of slaves to them at the end of every month. We made the promise; today we made the delivery. Tonight we celebrate." The Alb's jaw clacked shut, then open again. "It's as simple as that."

"As simple as that," Balzan repeated. He stared at the Alb, recalling Chato's charred, twisted body, Dhurn's fire-consumed hut, and Lomar's still, staring eyes. . . . It was an effort for him to lower his hand and remove the knife from the hole it was attempting to carve in the

32

Alb soldier's side. The Alb was gaping at him in horror. Balzan said, "What do these Kharns look like?"

"Kharnites," the Alb said, then paused. His yellow eyes took on a distant look. "They're tall men, scaleless like you, though their skin is tough and dark like ours. . . ." He held up an olive hand. "They have no tails, but their backs slope like an Alb's, and their legs are heavy and muscled. . . ." The Alb waved his hand, saying, "How can I explain? They have . . . *power*."

"Power."

Nodding eagerly, the Alb hunched forward. "Like the zanth, they seem to stalk . . . as though the world were theirs to hunt in. And among their men, there're rumors about their king and queen, and something called a blood stone. . . ." The creature grinned suddenly, showing off his bony teeth-ridge. "They'll learn though. They think *we're* their slaves, but they'll find soon enough that no one makes a slave of an Alb." He looked at Balzan meaningfully. "No one."

Balzan sat back and considered what the Alb had told him. It fit with the Teacher's appraisal of the situation; obviously, the Albs couldn't have developed a weapon like the neutron sword . . . and equally obvious was the fact that the Kharnites had filled the Albs with fear.

"Where did they take the Endorian prisoners?" Balzan asked.

"To Kharn, of course. Where else?"

"Of course," Balzan murmured. "And where is Kharn?"

The Alb lifted his shoulders, dropped them. "Somewhere to the north, beyond the Winter Range. I overheard one of the Kharnites saying it was a week's journey in one of their sky-boats."

"That's all you know?" Balzan asked quietly. He prodded the soldier with his knife. "You're certain?"

"One more thing. Their leader's name is Sha. Lord Sha." The Alb shifted his tail and blinked at Balzan warily. "And that's all. Why should I hold anything back? Telling you this makes no difference; you'll be dead before you leave the camp."

"Don't be too sure of it," Balzan said. He got to his

feet and gestured for the soldier to follow. Bracing himself with his tail, the Alb hauled himself upright. Erect, he came barely to the young man's shoulder.

"What will you do with me now?" the Alb asked. His yellow eyes peered at Balzan through the dusk; the drink-induced grogginess was wearing off, and the Alb was beginning to show signs of increased nervousness. "You'll kill me, won't you?"

"Not if you keep quiet."

The Alb snorted, and his eyes followed the motion of Balzan's knife as it waved him forward. Balzan stepped back to allow the Alb to pass in front of him, intending to sap the soldier with the handle of his knife once he'd turned his back. He never got the chance. With startling speed the Alb's tail snapped up and whip-cracked against Balzan's wrist, sending the knife flying. Before Balzan could brace himself, the Alb whirled and struck him a glancing blow in the throat, stunning him. Through a haze of pain Balzan saw the Alb start off at a dead run toward the camp, shouting for assistance. The nearest guards were reacting, climbing to their feet; answering shouts came from elsewhere in the compound. In a matter of moments the camp would be mobilized, and though most of the soldiers would be too drunk to be a threat, enough of them would still be sober—and Balzan would be dead.

Drawing himself upright and forcing the agony in his throat out of his mind, he unhooked the therb from its latch and swung it out. The whip flicked through the air; the barb seemed to reach out and slash downward across the running Alb's skull. The Alb's momentum stumbled him forward a few more steps, then he crashed into the ground head-first, his tail flicking once before stiffening. Cursing softly, Balzan trotted into the compound, winding the therb into a loop as he ran. A few hundred yards away a group of gaapurs paced and snorted, tethered to a rope strung between two yrrl trees; Balzan headed toward them, cutting through the camp at a diagonal, ignoring the guards getting up around him. Passing the smoldering remains of a cooking fire, he paused and

34

grabbed up a few of the red-hot brands, and holding them so that the flying embers wouldn't fly against his body, he ran on.

There were tents on either side of him, low affairs of hide and cloth rising only a few feet off the ground. Under the tents, he knew, were the circular trenches used by the Albs as barracks. As he ran he set fire to the tents, glad that there'd been no rain in the past week and that the hides were crisp and dry, ready tinder. The tents went up like bonfires, trapping the soldiers within them. Screams of terror and agony echoed behind Balzan as he left the compound and reached the paddock where the gaapurs were tethered. He smiled.

Smelling the smoke and seeing the flames licking upward only a few yards away, the gaapurs were on the verge of panic, their round orange eyes wide with fear, their nostril-slits blowing air, their horned hooves kicking the dry earth into dust clouds. Balzan slipped under the rope and moved among them, calming the beasts and untying their reins. He reached one gaapur—a shoulder-high mount with light brown fur and milky-gold eyes—that looked like the healthiest of the bunch, and made a special effort to gain the beast's confidence. The gaapur snorted and whined nervously until Balzan untied its reins and led it back from the makeshift corral; then it bumped its head against his shoulder and pressed its muzzle into his offered hand. "That's it," Balzan said. "That's it, you can trust me; I won't hurt you, that's it. . . ."

In the camp a few officers had managed to gain control of the hysterical soldiers, and were ordering them into action. A group of Albs was delegated the task of dosing the fires, and these soldiers hurried off to collect water from a nearby well. Balzan watched these proceedings as he took a saddle from a pile under one of the two yrrl trees; lifting it to his shoulder, he saw one of the officers start suddenly and point in his direction; he didn't wait to learn whether the officer had seen him or not; shouldering the saddle, he hurried back across the compound to his mount. Behind him he could hear a cry of command; what the cry said, he couldn't tell.

"Easy, now," he said, settling the saddle in place behind the gaapur's thick shoulder ridge. He swung into place on the gaapur's back, half-expecting the beast to throw him; instead the gaapur started from the camp at a trot, shifted to a cant, and at Balzan's urging broke into a fast gallop that soon left the Alb compound far behind.

Thirty seconds after he left, he was already being pursued.

2.

The Alb riders caught up with him in the foothills of the Winter Range, on a slope swept clean of shrubbery by a recent landslide. Balzan had dismounted and left his gaapur in a shallow cave on a ledge several yards above the slope, and he'd been waiting for his pursuers to arrive for almost fifteen minutes, wondering if they'd lost him in the forest at the base of the hill. Crouched between two slabs of rock over an overhang above the trail he'd taken, Balzan watched the fire in the Alb camp as it painted the dark night sky a brilliant orange and sent up plumes of rich gray smoke to mingle with the clouds, studying the scene with interest. From where he sat, the Alb soldiers were ants scurrying around a gutted anthill, trying vainly to repair what had been destroyed. He felt a warm satisfaction; though it could never bring back his dead fellows, the destruction of the Alb camp gave him a feeling of duty fulfilled. He smiled as he thought this; it wasn't a concept Lomar would have approved.

There was movement in the forest. Two riders broke from the foliage and charged their mounts into the clearing below the mountain. After a moment two more riders appeared, and the four Albs gathered to confer. Balzan debated whether he should give them a sign which would reveal his whereabouts and decided against it; it would be too obvious a move.

At last one of the riders started up the winding trail Balzan had taken to his present position. The other riders followed the first, leading their gaapurs in a single file up the treacherous mountain path. Balzan grinned while he waited for the first rider to pass beneath him. He felt a surge of excitement, an emotion he'd experienced previously only during a hunt, in the moment before the kill. It was a hot excitement, something that boiled in his blood. Leaning forward, he could see the lead rider's eyes studying the trail, yellow-gold eyes in an olive face. Inexplicably, the sight of the Alb's eyes sent a shiver up Balzan's spine.

Twenty seconds later the rider passed under Balzan's hiding place.

Balzan drew in a breath and kicked at the stone he'd lodged in the earth at his feet.

The stone broke free, taking with it a chunk of dirt and loose rock. The miniature landslide tumbled and spun past the ledge where Balzan sat, knocked more earth free on the next level, collected more rocks, suddenly became an avalanche plowing down the slope toward the Alb riders.

They never had a chance. It was over in an instant; a cloud of gray dust abruptly boiled up and over the riders, sweeping the gaapurs off the mountain and shoving the entire troop shrieking down the slope like a tidal wave cleaning a beach. Balzan watched the landslide until it thundered out at the base of the mountain, hundreds of feet below. He'd expected to feel exultation; strangely, he felt only a sick release.

Perhaps Lomar had been right.

Sometimes revenge wasn't sweet after all.

3.

An icy wind cut through his tunic, freezing his skin as he reined in his gaapur at the top of the pass through the Winter Range. He clutched his vest more tightly closed across his chest and stared at the vast plain stretching away into the misty distance, thinking about what lay before him and remembering what was already in his past. Between his legs the gaapur paced and snorted, complaining of the bitter cold and the two nights without rest;

gently, Balzan reached down and patted the beast's side affectionately. "When we reach the lowlands, I'll let you ride on *my* back. Just don't give in on me yet. Not yet." The gaapur blew air from its nostrils; the water vapor in the air formed crystals along its snout and crest. Balzan brushed them away without thinking.

Turning in his saddle, Balzan looked back at the valley he was leaving. Mist covered most of the land; the rest was too far away to be clearly visible. He couldn't make out details: the Alb camp, the Endorian village, the plain where his parents' spacecraft had crashed . . . they all seemed to blur together like a dimly remembered memory. Not even a memory: a dream.

But it wasn't a dream. Somewhere in the land lying north of him his sister and his tribesmen were being held captive; that was real and, at the moment, more than real.

Pressing his heels into the gaapur's sides, he started the beast down the path toward the land of Kharn.

Chapter Four

Already the storm was beginning to dissipate. The sky, washed by the twilight rain, appeared in pale green patches between drifting clouds, allowing the last rays of the evening sun to touch the uppermost spires of the city of Kharn. Here and there flecks of gold sparkled in the sunlight, marking windows and balconies situated at varying heights among the towers. Beneath the towers, however, the city was dark; the dying sunlight couldn't reach the twisting sidestreets of the Lower Town, and the garbage strewn alleys and intersections remained cloaked in night.

But above there was light, and in the light there was laughter.

The feast had been in progress for two days, and though he enjoyed the food and wine, Gamemaster Trito was beginning to find the endless music tedious. He watched the dancing slaves as they moved across the court, winding a sinuous path around the central fountain, and debated how he could best engineer an exit. Glancing over the assembled lords and ladies of Kharn, he could tell he wasn't alone in his boredom; he could count five other obviously disinterested faces among the nobility—one of the lords was even asleep, snoring loudly as he lay sprawled among his pillows and overturned goblets of wine. Trito looked toward the throne at the far end of the court and grimaced: the Red Lord was studying the slaves' dance eagerly, his withered lips twisted in a leer, his gnarled hand pounding out the rhythm of the drums on the ornate arm of his throne. The seat beside

Dragus was empty of course; his queen had little patience for these palace entertainments. She preferred the public fetes, Trito knew; Queen Myrane existed for the monthly bloodletting of the Games. So, for that matter, did he, but his interest was purely professional; hers was rooted in something far more primitive. . . .

He started when a hand touched his shoulder. Turning, he saw the pinched face of his personal slave, Whein, looking down at him. "Yes?" Trito said. "What is it now?"

"Lord Sha," said the slave. "He's been sighted, approaching from the south."

"Sha? He's returned, then?" Trito heaved himself to his feet, grunting as his unused limbs burned with the pain of renewed circulation. He ran a hand down the front of his formal vest and tunic, and straightened the fall of his billowing pants. "About time. He's been gone almost two weeks. It's never taken him this long before."

"Perhaps there are fewer slaves to be had, master."

Trito shot the slave a look, wondering if he'd detected a note of sarcasm in the smaller man's voice. It was difficult at times to read Whein's expression: he was heavily furred, and only his hands and part of his face were hairless. "Where is Lord Sha docking his ship?" Trito asked finally. The slave gave a grimace which barely resembled a smile.

"On the upper dock," the slave said. "The northwest terrace, above the arena."

"Have arrangements been made to receive the prisoners?"

"We wait on your command, master."

"Arrange it then," Trito drew himself up. "I'll make my apologies to the Red Lord and join you in a few minutes."

The slave bowed and backed away. Trito watched him shuffle off, then turned and walked across the court toward the throne.

He smiled.

They came like tethered birds across the sky, three large tubes filled with a gas that was lighter than air and drawn by cables attached to gaapurs on the ground below. From his vantage point on the palace tower Trito could see the tiny animals, burdened by the man-sized weights needed to hold them to the ground; still, the beasts moved without too much effort, guided by their drovers over the rough ground outside the city walls. Raising his eyes, the Gamemaster studied the ships drifting toward him. In the lead, of course, was Sha's personal craft, the *Starskimmer*, a tube almost two hundred feet long and decorated with a sculptured bird-woman on its prow, thirty feet high, whose wings curved back along the sides of the tube, thrusting her massive breasts forward. On either side of the flagship were the two ships of Sha's private fleet; neither was as ornate as the *Starskimmer*, but both were magnificent, rivaling the Red Lord's own. But *only* rivaling, Trito reflected; to do more would jeopardize Lord Sha's standing with his liege—and that was something Sha would never allow.

As the *Starskimmer* touched the outer end of the docking platform, the last clouds remaining from the storm parted, releasing a burst of sunlight across the towers of the city. Jerking twice, the sky-ship bumped to a halt. Slaves rushed onto the dock and gathered in the restraining cables and attached them to the metal loops spaced along the platform. Trito waited until the other two ships had docked and then strode across the open platform toward the *Starskimmer's* gangplank. A group of soldiers lowered the plank to the dock and hurried down it to take up their position at its base. A moment later Lord Sha appeared, the soldiers bowed, and Sha descended.

"My lord, we are blessed by your return." Trito inclined his head. "I hope your expedition was successful, and a glory to our lord?"

"Successful, yes. A glory?" Sha laughed. "That's for fools like you to decide."

He was a tall man, a pillar beside the squat Trito, dressed in armor polished to a mirror sheen, possessing hard, blunt features, cold brown eyes and thick shaggy green hair. Trito fell into step beside Sha as he crossed the dock toward the palace roof. As they walked Sha removed his helmet and ran a clawed hand through his hair. "It was ugly this time, Trito. We were forced to deal with a tribe of primitives. Vicious brutes; you'd like them. They'd make better gladiators than the slaves they found for us, I'd wager. They're quite a sorry lot, this batch. Food for the huulat, if you ask me."

"They sound promising, my lord."

Sha glared at him. "You'd think so. The citizens prefer the huulat slayings to an honest gladiatorial duel, don't they, Gamemaster?"

Trito shrugged. "So it seems, my lord."

"And as Gamemaster, you provide what the citizens prefer."

Trito smiled. "Precisely, my lord."

Sha snorted and spat, barely missing Trito's slippered foot. "It scarcely matters that *you* enjoy the huulat killings also, does it?"

With a look of injury, Trito said, "My lord, it matters not at all."

"I'm sure it does not." Sha brushed past Trito and took up a stance at the mouth of the ramp leading to the lower chambers of the tower, where the prisoners would be quartered. The guard standing before the entrance bowed, and Sha acknowledged the bow disinterestedly.

"Start the unloading," he said. The guard bowed again and shouted a command to the soldiers around the base of the sky-ships. Within moments the panels were removed from the cargo ports, planks were lifted into place and the prisoners were urged from the holds onto the dock. Each ship disgorged thirty prisoners, ninety-odd Endorians in all. The Cat-people milled about on the dock platform nervously as the soldiers checked their numbers against a cargo manifest. Satisfied that all the prisoners were accounted for, the soldiers began prodding them toward the ramp. Sha watched the operation with apparent distaste. Trito's expression was one of eagerness; noticing this, Sha grunted and shook his head.

"Dragus picked well when he chose you for Gamemaster," Sha said. The squat man blinked at him curiously and Sha went on. "You're a sadist, Trito. You enjoy inflicting pain on these wretches."

"But, my lord, it's you who carries an electro-prod," Trito pointed out quietly.

Sha glanced at the whip he held in his right hand. It had a thick base, a white button near his thumb; when pushed, the button engaged a circuit that sent a jolt of electricity through the barb of the whip. In concept it was similar to the Endorian therb, but in practice it was subtler and more cruel. Sha took the whip out and glanced at Trito.

"There's a difference. When I whip a prisoner, it's to make him move more quickly. The cruelty I inflict is in the service of efficiency. *Your* cruelty, Trito—"

"—Is in the service of the Red Lord," Trito finished, bowing.

For a moment Sha seemed on the verge of striking the stocky Gamemaster. Several seconds passed before the tall man relaxed and turned his attention back to the prisoners, passing before him in a line three across.

Abruptly Sha stepped forward and tapped the soldier nearest him. "I want three of those women to be added to my concubines. That one, and that, and this one here." He indicated three Endorian females as they approached. Nodding once, the soldier reached into the line and pulled the women aside. They were dressed in multicolored shifts, three separate bands of cloth wound around their torsos and caught by pins on their hips. Two of the women had silky tan fur, large heads, and bright luminous eyes; the third was a small, delicate female with golden fur and golden eyes. Sha pointed at her with the handle of his whip. "You. How many years have you?"

"Twenty." The girl looked at him incuriously. She seemed weary, somehow, exhausted. Sha pursed his lips and nodded.

"And your name?"

43

"Kitta," said the Cat-girl.

Sha studied her a moment longer, turned his gaze to the other two women, asked their names also, and when the questioning was done, said, "Have them brought to my quarters," and walked away.

3.

An hour later he was called before the Red Lord and his queen for his report.

The court had been cleared of all signs of festivity, the pool drained and refilled with clean water, the brightly colored drapes replaced by somber scarlet and black, the colors of the lord, and both Dragus and Queen Myrane were attired in formal robe and gown, as was Lord Sha. Sha entered and bent his knee in obeisance, and rose when Dragus made a negligent wave. His attention wasn't commanded by the Red Lord, however; it was held completely by the queen.

Her skin was the color of milk, and as smooth, her features were sharp and defined—arched eyebrows, a perfect nose, a delicate mouth—and her body beneath her gossamer gown was long and supple, a form evolved from a feline ancestor, not a lizard like Sha. She held herself regally, her back straight despite the reclining throne in which she sat beside the elderly Red Lord, her hands gripping the ornate arms of the throne with a mixture of sensuality and tension that made Sha uncomfortable when he noticed it. She watched him with amusement as he gave her a summary of the events of the expedition in clipped, precise language, and she smiled outright when he finished and asked if they required anything more.

"Tell us, Sha," she said, "do you find these new outlanders interesting?"

"In what way, my lady?"

"You say they are cat-evolved." She stretched herself sinuously. "Do such creatures excite you?"

"My lady!"

44

"Come, Lord Sha. Answer my question. Your queen commands it."

Sha said stiffly, "They neither interest nor excite me, my lady. They are slaves, no more."

Before he could exit, Sha was stopped once more as the queen leaned from her chair, her eyes bright and shining, and asked, "Have you taken any of the females, Sha? To add to your concubines?"

Sha closed his eyes, realizing what was to come. "Yes, my lady."

The queen clapped her hands in feigned delight. "Then you *do* find them exciting, Sha. You see, you lust after these cat-evolves after all!"

"No more," Sha said quietly, "than any other slave."

With that he bowed and strode quickly from the court. Behind him he heard the queen's laughter, and the Red Lord's half-whispered reply.

That night he thought of the Queen Myrane, and dreamed of her emerald eyes. He woke in a sweat and damned himself for a fool.

There was little else he could do.

"Wonderful, isn't it?" said the old man through
his smile.... For the first time, Balzan recognized the
thick odor of the filth and refuse lining the street, and
beneath it all he sensed...

Chapter Five

Balzan reached the city of Kharn on the morning of
the sixth day after he left Endore. He left his path-weary
gaapur at the entrance to the city, in a corral designated
for that purpose by one of the guards at the gate, and
entered Kharn with his pack slung over one shoulder and
his hand resting lightly on his blade.

At first he was stunned by the explosion of color and
sound. Everywhere he looked there were banners and
flags, strung across the street ahead, hung over doorways
and flying from poles beside merchants' stalls. Each banner bore a symbol, either a picture of an animal or plant,
or a group of markings Balzan couldn't read but supposed
were writings of some kind. He guessed they indicated
addresses, in much the same way as the Endorians used
figurines on plaques to mark places and names; even so,
the symbols were incomprehensible to him. Even more
incomprehensible were the sounds pounding around him:
the clangor of drums and flutes, the cacophony of voices
raised to a shout in order to be heard over the brutal
music, the thousand noises of a city alive. For several
seconds he remained near the gates, overpowered by the
blast of energy coming from the crowded, winding streets
ahead. One of the guards noticed him and strolled over,
grinning.

"From a township, aren't you?" the guard asked.

Not fully understanding the guard's question, Balzan
nodded vigorously. The guard's grin broadened and he
clapped the young man hard on the shoulder.

"It's a shock at first, I know," the older man said.

"Remember how it was for me, all these things to see, the smells—" For the first time Balzan recognized the thick *odor* of the city, mingled odors of burning grease and human sweat. The guard shut his eyes and laughed hoarsely. "But you'll learn to like it, lad. Soon you won't understand how you lived without it. Take my word, lad. Take my word."

Recovering from his initial reaction, Balzan let out a sigh. It was, after all, no worse than an earth city might be, and he'd seen pictures and tapes of all the major cities on earth; still, seeing and actually *experiencing* were two completely different matters. . . .

"Is there someplace I can find a bed?" he asked the guard, shouting to make himself heard.

"A bed? You want an inn, lad, and from the look of you, not a very expensive one." The Kharnite ran a hand along his blunt chin, frowning, the lizardlike lines of his face stretching out as he did. "I've just the place. Run by a friend of mine; not one of these cult fanciers, if you understand me." He elbowed Balzan knowingly; Balzan mimicked the guard's expression of worldly wisdom. "Three streets down, two over; it's the Banner of the Blue Root. You'll see it right off."

Balzan thanked him. The Kharnite shrugged. "Tell him I sent you. The name's Trull."

Again Balzan thanked the guard; the Kharnite laughed, shook his head and walked away. Unsettled, Balzan hurried on.

Slowly he realized what bothered him about the city, and wondered why he hadn't realized it earlier.

Kharn was structured on two levels, mutually exclusive. Light and dark, new and old, rich and poor, city and slum. He'd read about slums when he'd studied the tapes the Teacher had shown him of earth, but the tapes had portrayed the condition as something long past, an evil abandoned, a sickness cured. Yet Kharn, with a technology apparently equivalent to that of twenty-sixth century earth—to judge by the neutron-sword and the towers rising

47

from the center of this city—not only had not solved the problem of its ghetto; it wallowed in it.

What it was that brought him to this conclusion Balzan couldn't have said. It was a feeling he received, as though the people didn't *care* about their condition and were, in fact, completely apathetic. It was an emotion he'd never encountered before and it frightened him. He walked along the street in a near-daze, only partly aware of what he was seeing. It seemed unreal to him. He tried to block it out.

Children played in a gutter heaped with garbage, their clothes ragged and torn and splashed with mud and vomit. Near them their parents lolled about in the entranceways to decaying buildings, clutching flasks of wine and mumbling to each other in a language Balzan could barely make out. Twice he stumbled over what seemed to be a dead man but what turned out on closer inspection to be someone hopelessly drunk. Once he had to stop in an alley that stank of urine and feces, where he threw up until his stomach heaved and his eyes watered, and his knees went weak with reaction. And finally he reached the inn the guard had described, on a street that was brightly lit and lined with stalls and banners, and where the children were hidden in their houses at least, and their parents were *quietly* drunk.

There was a flag outside the tavern's broad window: on a red field a blue tree bloomed, surrounded by symbols Balzan was unable to read. He found the door and entered, leaving the sights and sounds and smells behind him and stepping into the near-silent and near-empty tavern, where he let out a breath of relief.

Placing a metal cup on the counter as Balzan approached, the innkeeper swept his gaze over the young man and poured him a drink from the flask of sarn he held in his right hand. "You've been sick? Have some of this. Always the same, you know. You towners come to the city and drink the water, and the next thing you know—that's it, lad, drink up."

Balzan downed the warm wine in two gulps, waited

while the innkeeper poured him another and swallowed that drink more slowly. The innkeeper took the cup back and tossed it under the counter. "Two credits, lad. Is there anything else you need?"

"A bed if you have one. A man named Trull told me to come here." Balzan took some coins from the saddle-bag he'd removed from his gaapur and tossed them on the counter. The innkeeper, a lean man with dull brown eyes and a long seamed face, picked up three of the coins and shoved the rest back.

"The bed'll cost you a credit," he said. He glanced at the coins, then peered at Balzan curiously. "These are military-minted credits, lad. Where'd you get them?"

Thinking of the Albs from whom he'd stolen the gaapur and its saddlebag, Balzan smiled and said, "From a friend." No doubt part of the Alb's payment for the Endorians had been in coin-of-the-realm, which raised some interesting questions . . . such as, would he find any Albs in Kharn who'd accompanied the sky-ships home, to enjoy their spoils? He asked the innkeeper and the lean man wrinkled his face, shaking his head.

"Never heard of them," he said, "which doesn't mean they aren't here. You looking for one in particular or just in general?"

"In general," Balzan answered. "I'm trying to find some friends of mine who were taken prisoner."

"By these Albs of yours?"

"Directly."

The innkeeper continued to shake his head. "Can't help you. Don't know why you'd look here, lad. There's no slave trade in Kharn, more's the pity."

"This wasn't precisely for trade," Balzan said slowly. "They were delivered to one of your noblemen. A Lord Sha."

At the mention of Sha's name the innkeeper's face went through a metamorphosis, from shock to suspicion, ending with an expression that mingled fear with shrewdness. "Sha, you say? Now that's a name I've heard, lad. So you want to meet the good Lord Sha, do you?"

"That's not what I said."

49

The Kharnite raised his hand and waved it. "Of course not. You're simply interested."

Balzan nodded. "Can you tell me anything?"

The other man shrugged. He wiped his hands on his leathery apron and came around the counter into the half-empty tavern proper to put an arm around Balzan's shoulders. "Hard to say. If I told you anything now it'd be premature, if you understand my meaning. How about this: you seem tired, and you've paid for a bed, so why don't we send you off to get a few hours' sleep while I put my nose into things, so to speak. By morning I'll have some information you can use, and we'll see what sort of—ah—fiscal arrangements we can make. You understand?"

"I see."

"Excellent." The innkeeper dropped his arm and stepped back, tucking his hands into the deep pockets of his apron. "You'll find a room at the top of the stairs, to the left as you enter the hall. Not much, but it's got a bed and a window for the night air, and some straw you can use if the mattress seems too thin. It should satisfy you."

Shouldering his saddlebag, Balzan thanked the innkeeper and started up the stairs. Halfway up he paused and turned around. The Kharnite looked up from behind his counter when Balzan called to him. "I meant to ask," Balzan said. "Why is this part of the city so filthy? How can you live with it?"

"What do you mean?" the innkeeper asked, lifting an eyebrow.

Balzan started to speak, noticed the lack of comprehension plain on the innkeeper's features, said, "Never mind," and took the remaining steps to the unlighted second floor.

2.

He woke quickly, as he'd been trained. An instant passed before the remains of his nightmare passed from him, but then he sat upright and swung his legs over the edge of the cot and listened for the sound which had pulled him out of his sleep, and as he listened it came again: a mutter of voices near the hallway stair.

He couldn't make out what was said, though he could tell there were more than two men speaking. He thought he recognized the innkeeper's husky tones, but he couldn't be sure. He didn't wait to find out. Rising to his feet, he started to pull his vest off the peg where he'd hung it before retiring that morning. He was about to slip it over his left arm when the door splintered open behind him and six armed Kharnites came barreling into the room.

In the moment it took them to orient themselves, Balzan had whirled and snatched his sword from its place beside his cot, and sent it arcing toward the nearest Kharnite, a fat, spraddle-legged man who gaped as his chest sliced open and screamed as Balzan carried his motion through. Blood sprayed over the hard wooden floor, mixing with the dry straw and dirt. His scream gurgling in his throat, the Kharnite crumpled into a dead heap. Balzan went over him and dove into the remaining soldiers, cutting and thrusting, ignoring the cries of pain and rage, seeing in his mind the remaining image of his nightmare—Chato's bloody face, her eyes dead and staring.

One of the Kharnites managed to free his sword from its sheath before Balzan reached him, and had it poised when the young man brought his own blade down in a cut that would have taken off the soldier's arm, had it connected. The two swords met in a shower of electricity, lightning flashing along their lengths, jolting both men into momentary shock. Balzan recovered first and thrust at the Kharnite soldier. The soldier avoided the thrust, parried Balzan's next blow and went in under the young man's guard. The soldier's sword passed within a quarter of an inch of Balzan's ribcage. Ducking back, Balzan managed to dodge the Kharnite's subsequent attack long enough to finish off the two other remaining soldiers, who stared stupidly at him until his sword went in and opened their lower abdomens.

Balzan turned and faced the surviving man. Neither had room to maneuver; the room was too narrow, the ceiling

51

too low, and a post in the center of the room broke the area into two sections. Balzan was in one "half" of the room, the Kharnite soldier occupied the other.

And behind the soldier was the room's only door.

For several seconds the two men stood glaring at each other, breathing in short ragged pants. Balzan's naked chest and thighs were gory with blood. The Kharnite was no prettier. It took Balzan a few moments before he could see past the blood spattering the man's face and make out the features under it.

"Trull!"

"The same," said the Kharnite tightly.

"I've no quarrel with you."

Trull gestured at the soldiers strewn at their feet. "You had no quarrel with them either, outlander."

"They came smashing into my room," Balzan said, shaken. "If that's not grounds for a quarrel, what is?"

"You forget: I came with them. See? We *do* have a quarrel after all."

Balzan shook his head. "I don't understand, Trull. Why did you attack me? What's the purpose behind all this?"

The Kharnite soldier's eyes narrowed. "My innkeeper friend reported you to my superior, outlander. He denounced you as an agent of our enemies, a spy; he said you made threats against Lord Sha, that you spoke treason against our city—"

"Your Lord Sha is responsible for the deaths of my countrymen," Balzan said, speaking quietly. "And he's taken members of my tribe as prisoners . . . and if saying as much is treason, then see it as treason. You *still* haven't explained what all this has to do with you."

"I let you pass the gate," Trull said. "That makes you my responsibility. *My* responsibility, outlander.

"It's my duty to see you die."

Balzan moved. In a lunge he'd grabbed up his clothes; in another lunge, using the bed as a springboard, he dove through the open window above his cot and tumbled two stories to the ground below. Like a cat, he landed on his feet. Trull shouted from the window; an answering shout came from the alley mouth twenty feet away. Re-

52

gaining his balance, Balzan shot a glance toward the street. There were ten soldiers there, unsheathing their swords as they started toward him. In the opposite direction there was a brick wall at the alley's end half again as tall as a man. There were no other doors leading into the tavern or the building beside it; no other exits at all.

Naked, his clothes in one hand and his sword in the other, he took four running strides down the alley away from the soldiers, and on the fourth stride sprang. He hit the top of the brick wall hard on his ribcage, grunting as the breath slammed out of him. Then he threw himself over the wall, dropped down, and found himself on a deserted side street. He spent ten seconds clambering into his pants and vest. Dressed, he sprinted through the darkness, listening as the sounds of pursuit grew fainter behind him, finally smiling as he turned a corner and fell into a shadowy doorway. For the time being, he'd escaped.

For the time being, he was free.

3.

The tavern was part of a larger building, an aged tower half as tall as those glistening new buildings in the center of the city. Some of the windows in the upper stories of were dark. At the base of the building, however, there was light—a dirty yellow light, filtering through the grimy tavern window to cast a rectangular glow on the cracked pavement of the walk. As Balzan approached the building, he heard voices and music. The door of the tavern opened, light spilled out, two burly Kharnites staggered through the doorway, laughing and clapping each other on the back, and the door swung shut behind them. Balzan stepped up and caught the door before it could close completely. Sound blasted out at him. He moved inside.

It was a larger tavern than the inn where he'd spent the day. Seventy feet across, it had two levels: a wooden platform running around a central court where men jostled each other around a circular bar, drinking from large-handled mugs, and a pit to the rear where a group of five

53

musicians sat on stools, playing woodwinds just barely loud enough to be heard over the general noise. He stood on the platform just beyond the entrance and got his bearings. There were tables on this platform, crude wooden affairs large enough for ten men to sit around, but the tables nearest him were crowded with Kharnites and stacked high with empty mugs. He found a table with one vacant seat halfway around the platform. Shoving his way past the men crowding the edge of the platform, he reached the spot and slid into the empty chair. The other men at the table ignored him.

He was craning his neck, looking for a serving wench or a slave, when a hand touched his shoulder and a voice above him said, "That's my seat, farmer. Do you get up, or do I snap your neck?"

Startled, Balzan half-turned and faced a Kharnite who appeared slightly older than he was, a sturdy, handsome man who looked at him from under a tangle of black hair, with eyes just a shade darker than sand. "*Your* seat? There was no one here when I came by," Balzan said. "And if these are your friends, they didn't speak up for you."

"An honest mistake, then," said the sandy-eyed man. "Let's not compound it."

About to reply, Balzan broke off at a sound from the street. Soldiers. He heard the clatter of gaapur-hooves, men shouting at one another, the grating tones of an officer giving commands. His face must have reflected Balzan's anxiety, for the young Kharnite's features suddenly shifted from an expression of annoyance to one of concern.

"You're in trouble?"

Balzan nodded. "Come with me," the Kharnite said.

He tightened his grip on Balzan's shoulder and pushed the young man ahead of him through the crowd toward the rear of the tavern. "Keep your head down," the Kharnite whispered in Balzan's ear. "They won't see you if you keep your damned brown head down!" Balzan complied, ducking forward as he weaved through the knot of men on the upper platform. They came to a stair leading down to the lower level, and the Kharnite urged

Balzan to take it. He did, and they passed through the men gathered there more quickly than they'd passed through the drinkers above. Balzan was picking up the urban style of shouldering through mobs.

The door of the tavern slammed open and soldiers flooded the room. Immediately the soldiers began to thrust the drinkers back against the walls of the tavern, clearing a path by smashing heads together and knocking bodies out of their way. Balzan glanced back and saw, to his surprise, that the Kharnites were accepting the brutality without complaint. Meekly, the men stumbled back, jerking their hands up to protect their faces, like children fearing a parental reprimand. The young Kharnite with him caught Balzan's look and said grimly, "I know. There's nothing we can do for them. Keep moving."

Reaching the musician's pit, Balzan was astonished to find it empty. He jumped down into the pit when the young Kharnite shoved him, and was about to turn and ask what they were doing there when he realized he was standing seven inches from an open trapdoor. "The musicians use it when they're changing between acts," the Kharnite explained. "It leads to the basement. Go on. Climb down."

Stunned into silence, Balzan dropped to his stomach and slipped through the trapdoor, found footing on a ladder rung and clambered into the pitch blackness below. After several rungs his foot touched stone flooring. He checked his footing carefully, still unable to see properly in the darkness, then stepped back from the ladder to allow his newfound friend to join him.

Above them, the soldiers were cursing; there were muffled thuds, a few cries of pain from an unfortunate drinker as the soldiers pressed their search.

Around them, there was silence.

"What now?"

"Now," said the Kharnite, "we go underground."

Chapter Six

"We'll be relatively safe here," the Kharnite, whose name was Lio, said. He swept a hand about, indicating the empty room and gutted windows, open to a view of the city's northern slums. "We can talk."

"You know this part of Kharn pretty well, don't you?" Balzan asked.

"I've lived here most of my life."

Balzan shook his head as he found himself a place to sit amidst the rubble. "That's something I can't understand. People actually staying in this slum, with the entire world waiting outside. Why do you do it?"

Lio shrugged. "It's home, I suppose. At least, it is for me."

"I see," said Balzan, and he did. It was an emotion he could sympathize with, for it echoed his own feelings for Endore, and, yes, his attachment to the world of his birth, a planet he'd never seen. He studied Lio thoughtfully. For a while he'd thought of Kharnites as being somehow inhuman, yet here was a man who felt about his land the way Balzan felt about his own; in addition, the man had helped him. That indicated something, didn't it? Oddly, Balzan couldn't be sure what.

He gazed around the room Lio had led him to. The walls were stained and filthy, paint peeling back from the beams in long curling strips, the wood underneath decayed and diseased. There were remnants of furniture scattered across the floor, broken chairs, a table with one leg missing propped against the far wall, a mound of dust and rotting cloth in a corner, rain-bleached clothes near Bal-

zan's feet. The place stank of corruption, of dirt and
the tower were broken or missing; all of the windows
urine, and other, fouler things. It was hard for Balzan
to conceive of people living in such squalor at one time;
with a shock, he realized that some Kharnites probably
still did.

Lio bent and picked up a stubby brown candle, lit it
and placed it on a shelf jutting from the wall near the
northern window. The candlelight lit the room poorly, but
well enough for Balzan to make out his rescuer's features
and expression. Lio was smiling.

"So tell me," the Kharnite said. "Why were those
soldiers hunting you?"

"What's more interesting is why you saved me."

Lio spread his hands. "An honest man does what he can
for a stranger in trouble. The question is, why were you
in trouble? I'd like to know something about a man whose
skin I've saved from flaying."

Slowly Balzan told him. Lio's expression went from one
of interest to anger, finally became a look of disgust. By
the time Balzan had finished the Kharnite was pacing the
room, his rage more than apparent.

"It's for the Games, you know. Your friends will be
thrown into the arena, and that's the last we'll see of
them—though perhaps we'll see more of them than we
wish to, in the last moments they remain alive."

"I don't understand."

"You're an outsider; you wouldn't." Lio appeared distracted. He waved a hand impatiently. "There's nothing
we can do for them now, of course. Once the Gamemaster
gets his hands on you, you're finished."

"What do you mean?"

Lio looked at him, frowning. "It's the Games, Balzan.
Once a month our lords and masters invite the people
of Kharn to the palace garden, where they feast like pigs,
dance, and make love. And after the festival there are
the Games. On the roof of the palace the Red Lord has
erected an arena, an amphitheater large enough to seat the
entire population of Kharn. There the citizens of this city
find their entertainment watching the death struggles of

the yarrotites, who are trained to duel in bloody style, and the massacre of those unfortunates too weak or clumsy to be trained—and instead of fighting, are given to the huulat for slaughter. Have you ever seen a huulat, Balzan? You'll be sickened when you do. It's a monster, a beast apart from nature. It has an appetite twice that of a normal beast its size; and, Balzan, it is immense. Your friends won't last two minutes in the arena. Believe me, I know; I've seen what a huulat can do."

Balzan found that he was shaking, trembling with contained anger. "There's nothing we can do?"

"Nothing."

"I see," Balzan said. He got to his feet and started toward the sagging doorway. Lio came up behind him and took his arm.

"What are you doing now?"

Jerking free of the Kharnite's grip, Balzan ducked under the door and stepped into the hall. "If you don't want to help me, that's fine. I'll go by myself."

"Help you? Are you insane? How can I help you, how can any of us do *anything?*" Lio hurried after him, the two of them sidestepping around the debris cluttering the corridor. "My friend, I saved your life. What more do you want from me?"

Balzan paused at the head of a crumbling stairway. His face, lit from the side by moonlight through a grimy hall window, was empty of all expression.

"Nothing," he said quietly. "Nothing at all."

With that he drew away. He was halfway down the stairs before Lio caught up with him.

"All right," the Kharnite said, his voice weary. "There are some friends of mine you should meet. Come along."

Balzan moved aside and let Lio lead the way.

2.

They waited in the doorway of an abandoned building as a troop of soldiers passed, then Lio crossed the street and Balzan followed, the two of them moving from one pool of darkness to another, avoiding the circle of light surrounding a street lamp near the walkway. Balzan took note of the path, in case he and Lio became separated. The Kharnite strode down an alley, turned a corner and went up a flight of garbage-encrusted steps, under a stone arch and into a small courtyard. The windows of the buildings overlooking the courtyard were dark; the moonlight didn't reach here, and Balzan found himself straining his eyes futilely to see through the blackness. He heard metal scrape against stone, something clatter in the shadows ahead; a moment later Lio called out in a half-whisper and Balzan moved forward. He felt the Kharnite's hand on his arm.

"Be careful, there's a drop."

"A drop?"

"Get down on your knees. That's it. Reach out; do you feel it?"

"Yes. It's an opening."

"Grab the sides and lower yourself down. I'll follow and replace the cover."

His eyes adjusting to the dark, Balzan saw a circular hole before him. He swung his legs over the edge, held the rim, and dropped through. He hung for a few seconds from the opening, not sure how far he'd have to fall. Finally he released his hold. The floor was two feet below. He stumbled into an inch of fetid water and sprawled, catching himself with his hands. As he was getting to his feet he heard Lio land beside him. Overhead the metal cover clattered back into place.

"Where are we?"

"One of the sewer tributaries," Lio explained. Balzan noticed he was coiling a length of rope which had been attached to the cover and no doubt had jerked it into place over the hole. "The entire city is undermined by them."

"Is this what you meant by 'underground'?"

"In a manner of speaking." Lio tucked the rope into his belt and glanced in both directions up and down the tunnel. "This way," he said. Balzan followed a few steps behind the Kharnite, listening to the sound of water dripping in the tunnel, aware of the echo of their footsteps splashing through the shallow sewer river. Not for the first time, he wondered why Lio had rescued him. His newfound friend was more mysterious than he wished to appear.

Minutes passed as they negotiated the twisting tunnels and basins of the sewer, and Balzan soon lost hope of being able to retrace his steps. There were so many side passages, so few sources of light, that he began to feel as though he were wandering through a dream, one of those endless nightmares in which one is hunted and tracked, lost in eternal darkness. He'd spent his entire life in the open, or in the forests of his adopted homeland, and the city was a jungle terrifyingly new to him. He was beginning to doubt his ability to cope with its mysteries. He shivered, then drew himself together. He couldn't afford to lose control of himself, not here and not now. His tribesmen depended on him.

He *must* remain free.

Abruptly the tunnel before him was flooded with light. Distracted by his thoughts, Balzan was slow to react; he threw up his hands to shield his eyes just a minute too late—he was blinded.

Hands grabbed him from either side and he responded instinctively. He ducked, swung around and jerked free of the fingers restraining him. Someone cried out to his right and he thrust his fist forward, planting it firmly in a fleshy solar plexus. There was a grunt, a splash, and in the next instant four men landed on Balzan, bearing him down and knocking him into unconsciousness.

His last thought was one of dismay, that he'd let himself be so easily betrayed.

3.

He came to in a large chamber lit by torches set in niches in the walls. He was on a ledge jutting over the sewer water, lying on a mat of straw and leather a few feet from a smoky fire. Men ringed the fire, standing and staring at him with displeasure. Sitting up, Balzan saw Lio standing to one side. The Kharnite's arms were folded and his expression was a mixture of annoyance and amusement. When he saw that Balzan was awake, Lio said, "If you'd wanted to make your own introductions, why didn't you simply say so? You're a master of it, you know."

It took Balzan a second to realize what the Kharnite meant. He flushed and said, *"These* are—?"

"—my friends," Lio finished. "But of course, you've already met."

"I'm sorry. I didn't . . ."

"You didn't think, outlander," said one of the men squatting behind the fire. He was heavy-set, bearded, and one-eyed. "But don't feel bad about it. Few men think these days."

"Why'd you bring him here, Lio?" asked another man, older than the rest. "What sort of a thief will an outlander make? We'd have to teach him everything: where the jewels are, how to break into a private house, *everything.*" The old man spat into the fire. "You should have let the soldiers take him, I say. One less fool to worry about, one less mouth to feed."

Balzan gaped. He looked from one Kharnite to another, ended up gazing at Lio. "Thieves? You're thieves?"

"Of a kind," Lio said. "Some of us, at any rate."

"But from what you said, the way you talked . . ."

"You thought me a revolutionary?" Lio laughed. "In a way I suppose I am. We all are. Thieves and revolutionaries aren't *too* far apart, my outlander friend. These days one must be the other to survive. Oppression makes odd sleeping companions, wouldn't you say?"

"But *thieves* . . ."

"Don't get high and mighty," the heavy-set man said. "You're not in the outlands now. Things are different here. A man has few options in Kharn; fewer if he's the honest sort. And here at least we're all honest men."

"I say throw him to the soldiers." The old man hacked and spat again. "He'll just give us trouble, and he's no use to anyone the way he is now."

61

"You see?" Lio said, grinning. His teeth were sharp and pointed. "You're the center of controversy."

"Did you tell them why I'm here? Did you tell them about my tribesmen?"

"He told us everything while you slept, outlander," said the one-eyed man. "What's it to us?"

"I don't understand. Men and women are going to be killed. Don't you care?"

"They're not *my* men and women, outlander."

Balzan got to his feet. "I'm not going to waste time trying to convince you. Lio, thanks again for helping me, and thanks for bringing me to your . . . friends. If you'll show me the way out of this stink-hole, I'll see if I can find some *men* to aid me. I certainly won't find any here."

"Watch your tongue, boy." The heavy-set man heaved himself upright and towered over Balzan. His one good eye was bright with restrained anger. "Insulting us won't do you any good."

"I made no insult," Balzan replied. "I simply spoke the truth. A man would help me; a man would fight for his life and the lives of others. You won't; therefore, you aren't."

He turned away. He heard the heavy-set man snort in anger and start toward him. He waited until he sensed the man rearing up behind him; he whirled and drove his fist upward into the man's bearded chin, connecting with a solid-sounding *crack*. The bearded man stumbled backward and landed squarely in the fire. Howling, he shoved himself out of the flames, twisted and plunged into the sewer water. The other men blinked in astonishment. Lio started to laugh.

"Remember what I said," Balzan told them. "Live with it if you can."

"Don't go," Lio said, laughing. "I think we're satisfied now, aren't we?"

To Balzan's surprise, the men ringing the fire were nodding and mumbling assent. Lio spread his hands and smiled. "I'm sorry if we upset you, Balzan, but we had to be certain of your intentions. We have no need of a man who can easily be put from his purpose. That kind of man could endanger us all."

"Then this was a test?"

The Kharnite shrugged. "If you want to call it that, yes."

Balzan shook his head. "You and your friends have a great deal of nerve."

"I know," Lio answered, chuckling. He sobered suddenly. "But, as you can see, we survive.

"Above all else, my outlander friend, we survive."

Chapter Seven

Outside the palace window the sky was a dark deep green, unbroken by the light of the twin moons, which had set for the evening an hour before. There were no clouds in the sky; the night was cool and still. A gentle wind caught the fragrance of flowers on a distant hill and brought it wafting across the rooftops, taking it at last to the balcony where a young Endorian stood gazing at the towers below. She lifted her head, touched by the floral scent; her veil fell to her shoulders, revealing her soft, gleaming fur, a slope of neck, eyes that were bright and yet somehow terribly sad. She pulled the veil tightly about her shoulders and turned, passing through the open glass doors and stepping down into the apartment she shared with twenty other females. Most of them were asleep, curled on pillows placed here and there in the chamber. Two females were awake and talking in hushed tones under a shelf filled with small bottles of perfume and several large plants. The Endorian ignored them and crossed to her own pillow beside a decorative column. She lowered herself onto the makeshift bed, shut her eyes and tried to fall asleep.

A hand on her shoulder woke her.

"We want to talk with you," the more mature of the two females she'd seen talking said. She was of a race the Endorian had never seen before: pale-skinned, bright fur covering her skull, torso and limbs, her face and hands pink and bare. Her eyes were red points in pink; her mouth, though small, filled with sharp, vicious teeth. The other females called her Scala, the Hungry One. The

Endorian didn't doubt the appropriateness of the nickname; she'd heard stories among the females of the way Scala treated new "recruits," and the stories had made her shudder. Scala herself affected the Endorian no less strongly.

"I've done nothing against you," the Endorian said.

"I know," the older woman replied. She bared her teeth. "I want to make certain you never do."

"You have my word."

"What is your word to me?" Scala laughed. "Your fear —now, that's something you can offer that I'll accept. I'll take your fear, outlander. Are you willing to give it?"

The Endorian shivered. "Yes."

"What, so easily?" Scala grinned at her companion, who returned the leer. "That won't do, child. You must be taught properly. Nothing so brutal as to enjoin the Lord Sha's displeasure for ruining one of his concubines, of course. But there are . . . things we may do, tricks Fayra has learned, which have proven adequate in the past."

The other female smacked her lips. She was of a race related to the Albs, lightly scaled, with long, sinuous limbs that ended in bitter claws, heavy haunches and a wicked-looking tail. Like her Alb relatives, she had no teeth. Instead she possessed two ridges of sharp bone, which she clacked together as she leered at the trembling Endorian.

"Fayra is as entertaining as she is efficient," Scala said. "I'm sure you'll be amused."

The young Endorian looked from one female to the other. Her face cracked open and she screamed and lunged between them, leaping past the two startled women before either could react. Scala cried out; Fayra hissed. Both jumped after the Endorian and caught up with her as she scrambled at the locked door of the chamber. There was a moment's struggle before the Endorian was subdued. The two females were dragging her toward the center of the chamber when the door slammed open and three soldiers entered, followed by the squat lieutenant in charge of Lord Sha's household. The scene froze into a tableau; then the Endorian broke from her two assailants and flung herself at the lieutenant's feet, sobbing. He glanced at her, shot an enraged look at Scala and the panting

Fayra, bent and took the Endorian's arm, and led her from the room. The soldiers remained after the lieutenant had left, waited half a minute and exited, slamming the heavy door shut behind them.

Scala began to curse, loudly and in several languages.

2.

"Your name is Kitta, is it not?"

The Endorian female nodded. She kept her eyes on the floor near the Kharnite's slippered feet. Beneath her fur her skin was pale and mottled, her chest heaving as she fought to regain her breath. The Kharnite studied her, his lips pursed.

"You realize that Scala will want to kill you after this. You've embarrassed her before her peers; and more, you've brought yourself to my attention, a capital crime in Scala's book. You're in a fine state now, aren't you?"

"Yes, my lord," Kitta said.

"My Lord Sha," the Kharnite corrected.

"Yes, Lord Sha."

"That's better. If I'm to be your protector, you must learn to address me properly."

Neither said anything for several heartbeats. Lord Sha, dressed in a silk robe and slippers, had been wakened by the clamor in the concubines' quarters and had come to the barracks room to learn the reason for the commotion. He and Kitta were alone in the room now, Lord Sha having dismissed the lieutenant and the other house soldiers upon his arrival. They sat at opposite ends of the mess table, Lord Sha with his feet upon the bench, Kitta with her hands tucked demurely beneath her veils. The room was warmed and lit by a fire in a hearth facing the mess table; the fire formed shadows which flickered across Sha's face, and the girl's as well. When neither spoke, the room was as quiet as a tomb.

"What shall I do with you, Kitta? I can't send you back to the others; that's plain. Have you a suggestion?"

"Whatever my Lord Sha wills," Kitta said.

The Kharnite grunted. "Have you no will of your own? Or are you as resigned as you seem?"

"My lord?"

"Never mind. Perhaps you are; it doesn't matter." Sha slapped his hand on the table top decisively. "From this point until I order otherwise, you're my personal slave. You'll reside in a chamber off my quarters, and you'll be available to me at any time during the night or day. I'll issue orders that the guards are to protect you from attack by Scala or her friends. That's the best I can do."

"My Lord Sha is too kind."

"And you, my dear woman," Sha said, rising to his feet, "are incredibly lucky. Another night, I may have let you die, or killed you myself for disturbing my rest."

Kitta looked up, her face expressionless. "But tonight, my lord?"

Sha paused in the archway and frowned. "Tonight is different. It's not for you to know why, but tonight . . ." He broke off and grunted again. "We've talked too much already. I'll speak to the lieutenant; he'll show you your room. Get as much sleep as you can. No doubt I'll have need of you in the morning."

With that, he was gone. To her surprise Kitta found that she'd stopped shaking.

She couldn't have said why.

3.

A thin Kharnite slave in green silk robes was waiting for Sha when he returned to his chambers. The slave rose from the lounge he'd been sitting on and bowed as Sha entered the room. Sha returned the bow with a curt wave and said, "Will she see me or not? If not, say so and leave. I've no patience for excuses or apologies, not this night." It was a pretense, Sha knew; he would never have spoken that way if she'd been there; he wouldn't have considered it. The slave, however, was another matter. Slaves were created for abuse, by Sha's way of thinking. For abuse, and in the case of female slaves, for pampering and pleasure. This wasn't something Sha questioned; it was something he accepted instinctively. It was, after all, the only way he knew.

"The queen sends her greeting," the slave said. "She grants your request for a private audience, and begs you come in fifteen minutes' time."

"Fifteen minutes?" Sha laughed harshly. "Now who's the impatient one?" He gestured at the slave, who straightened up. "Tell your mistress I'll be with her shortly. Give her *my* greeting."

The slave bowed and left. Sha grunted and crossed the wide foyer to his private room, where he proceeded to wash and dress.

He arrived at the queen's apartment thirty seconds early.

Myrane stood at a marble table, pouring ruby-red wine into a large glass goblet. She glanced up at Sha as he moved through the beads curtaining the entrance to her bedchamber, and she smiled at him languidly when he made his formal greeting. She lifted the goblet, letting the wine catch the light from the lamp behind her. "Would you like wine?" she asked. She handed him the decanter and indicated an array of empty goblets. "You'll have to serve yourself, milord. I allow no slaves in my private quarters; the sight of them disturbs me."

A moment later they tapped their glasses together, then drank. Sha found the wine sweet and burning, with a bitter aftertaste. Myrane noted his expression; her laughter was soft and gently chiding.

"It's a special blend," she explained, "developed in my homeland. I enjoy it, but few Kharnites do. There is other wine on the chest near the window. If you wish, you may drink it instead.

"Now," she said, after Sha had filled his glass with sarn, "tell me about these new prisoners, Sha. Are they strong? Will the men fight?" She wet her lips and leaned forward, balancing herself with a delicate hand on the marble table top. She wore a filmy silk gown, a necklace of emeralds, rubies and glistening yellow stones. The gems seemed to catch the light reflected in her green eyes, refracting it and capturing Sha's gaze. He drew himself up finally, frowning.

"It's hard to say, my queen. As I've told Trito, they seem weak-willed, dispirited. In time it may pass, but for the moment—I'd say no, there isn't a potential yarrotite in the lot of them."

Myrane's face underwent a sharp transformation, from gentle interest to restrained rage. "Twice in one month you've returned with weakling captives. This does not please me, Sha. It will not please the Red Lord. And it most definitely will not please the citizens of Kharn."

"The citizens of Kharn prefer seeing the captives slaughtered by the huulat, milady."

"They prefer what I *say* they prefer: nothing more, certainly nothing less . . . *milord.*"

Sha's face tightened. "Of course. I meant no disrespect. If it will please you, I'll leave in the morning to explore the eastern lands." He set his goblet on the table, started to execute a bow, but stopped at Myrane's impatient gesture.

"Don't act like a hurt child," she said. "Gods, but you're an exasperating man." She pursed her lips and studied him critically. Sha noticed that her face was flushed, pinker than usual; he credited it to her anger. He bore her stare for almost a full minute and was on the verge of turning on his heel and stalking from the room, when he was startled to see her face flow into a smile, and startled even more to hear her laughter. She held her arms open to him. "Come here," she said. Her eyes seemed to glow in the semidarkness. "This *is* what you want, isn't it? It's what you've been thinking of all these weeks and months, it's what I saw in your eyes when you reported the other day. Very well, my lord, it's yours."

"I'm afraid I don't . . ."

"Try not to be an idiot," she said quietly.

He stepped forward hesitantly. "The Red Lord?"

"All I ask of him is his power," Myrane whispered. "For love, I must turn to men."

Sha moved into her embrace, wonderingly. Myrane tightened her arms around him, pressing her hands and

69

fingers into his back. Her voice vibrated against him as she whispered against his neck, "And if you're nothing else, don't be gentle."

4.

Smoke fogged the tower room, issuing from the grating of a brazier near a heavy wooden chair. The man in the chair listened to his servant's report attentively, nodding from time to time, tapping his fingers together over his lap. When the servant had finished, the man in the chair said, "Excellent. You may go," and raised his gnarled hand in dismissal.

The servant backed to the doorway and paused, obviously reluctant to leave. "Are there any orders for the palace guard?"

"None. Should there be?"

Anxiously, the servant shook his head. "I didn't mean to presume, master, I only . . ."

"I understand," the old man said. "But you see, her body is nothing to me. She can't take from me what she's never given. Let Sha have it if he must; I bear him no ill will. I have other uses for Myrane, and she for me."

"Forgive me, my lord."

"On your way," the Red Lord said. He glanced at the late-setting moon, visible through the smoke and the balcony windows. "It's time I went to sleep."

Silent, the servant backed from the room. The smoke went swirling with him.

Chapter Eight

From his vantage point on the ledge below the window, Balzan could see the room was dark and empty. He held himself against the outside wall beneath the sill, waiting for his eyes to adjust to the gloom broken by the candlelight from the stand in the center of the room, and listening to Lio's labored breathing coming from the ledge below. Against his better instincts, he chanced a look downward, saw the street sprawled a remote two hundred feet away, and jerked his head around again. Lio had warned him about looking down. The Kharnite had been right; though it was less strenuous physically, climbing in a city was infinitely harder than in Balzan's native forest. For one thing, the proportions of things were all wrong, the edges too sharp, the towers too slender and high. For another, the ground looked *hard;* forest ground seemed softer, covered as it was with leaves and earth. To his amazement and chagrin, Balzan was having his first encounter with acrophobia . . . and he was terrified.

"Keep moving," Lio whispered urgently. "Do you want someone to look up from the street and see us hanging here? Go over the sill, dammit. You can get ill *inside* the apartment."

Steeling himself, Balzan tightened his grip and hauled himself over the sill and dropped to the floor inside. Lio followed. The two of them squatted in the darkness beneath the chest-high window and glanced around the room. There were tables everywhere, most of them marble, some of them polished wood. All were covered by white sheets; one of them held the burning candle; the rest bore figurines, bowls, dozens of tiny statues—more art than Balzan had ever seen collected in a single place. From the hall doors came the sounds of conversations. There was a party going on in the next room, according to Lio's information. No one would see or hear the two of them, there'd be no witnesses, nothing to tie either Balzan or Lio to the crime. For it *was* a crime. Balzan was about to become a thief.

Lio led the way across the room to the cache, a niche in the wall behind a flat screen which showed an embroidered pattern in copper and gold on a white background: a huulat attacking slaves in the arena. Balzan took the picture from Lio after he'd removed it from the wall. Balzan gaped at the scene depicted on the screen. He knew about the huulat slayings, had accepted the concept intellectually, but had never seen one. The sight of it sickened him.

Twice Lio had to whisper his name before Balzan shook himself out of his reverie. The young Kharnite had opened the cache and was holding out a bag of coins. Balzan took the pouch and slipped it into the sack he was carrying over his shoulder. There were six bags altogether, each weighing two pounds. The total weight dragged his side down, unbalancing him.

"Is that it?" he asked. Lio nodded and replaced the embroidered screen. The two of them slipped back the way they came, negotiating the tables like two dark-clothed wraiths. Lio reached the window first, and was lifting himself over the sill when the door to the room opened and light exploded around them.

The Kharnite in the doorway was speaking to someone over his shoulder. He broke off and gaped at Balzan, who stood near the window, paralyzed. The Kharnite lord was impeccably dressed in red silk and fur, his robes tailored to conceal his heavy paunch, his hair long and well-groomed; his face blanched to a paler shade of green and he opened his mouth to scream, but before he could make a sound the Kharnite collapsed, struck down by the figurine Balzan had instinctively caught up from a nearby table and hurled when he saw the lord's mouth start to open.

"Don't stand there with your eyes bulging out," Lio shouted from the window. "Come *on,* dammit, *come on."*

Kharnites were milling in the doorway, crowding around the fallen, bleeding lord, staring at Balzan in confusion and fear. Balzan caught a glimpse of a heavy-set Kharnite in a military tunic shouldering his way through the press, and then he whirled and dove for the window. He scraped his legs as he swung over the sill, but he ignored the flash of pain. Lio had already clambered down to the ledge. Balzan came after him, moving awkwardly because of the sack on his shoulder.

"What do we do now?" he called.

"We get away from here as quickly as possible," Lio replied. "What do you think?"

Balzan didn't answer. He heard voices begin to shout and cry out above him, and the sound acted like a surge of adrenalin in his blood. He landed on the side of the roof directly below the ledge and ran lightly along the sloping tiles, chasing Lio's receding shadow. The young Kharnite leaped across the chasm separating one roof from another; Balzan made the leap with him. The coins clattered and jingled against his back with each running footstep he took; for some reason the sound was like laughter, cold chill laughter, mocking him as he ran beneath a moonlit sky.

"We can't spend it ourselves, of course," Lio said. He poured a handful of coins back into the pouch, leaving a few on the hard wood table. "That's where Fahl comes in. He'll make us a fair trade. He and I have worked together before; we can trust him."

Balzan sat up straighter. They were in the back room of a tavern Lio had brought them to, a squalid, low-ceilinged hovel that stank of grease and burning meat. Balzan pushed away the wooden plate of food he'd been eating and took a drink from the mug of wine that'd come with the food. "Why can't we spend it? It's money, isn't it?"

"Yes, but it's not *our* kind of money, my friend. It's patrician money." Lio held out a coin, which caught the lantern light and reflected it. "Do you see the inscription?

73

Can you read it? Neither can I. A patrician could, but that's not the point. *This* is a coin of the street—" he held up a dull gray slug "—but *these* are coins of the upper class. If we tried to spend one down here, we'd not only lose our money . . . we'd lose our heads."

"But this Fahl; he can spend it?"

"Let's simply say he has connections in the towers." Lio flipped the coin he held, caught it and slapped it on the table top. He lifted his hand and grinned. "When I play this with myself, I always win. When I game with another . . ." He shrugged, and his grin turned wry. "Fahl will give us street money for the patrician money; not as much as it's worth, but enough for our purpose."

Balzan drank some more wine. "What *is* our purpose, Lio?"

"To buy weapons, of course. What did you think our purpose was?"

"I'm not sure." Balzan lowered his mug to the table deliberately. "I've been with you for two weeks now, and all I've heard is talk. This is the first night we've been out, and instead of making an attempt to free the arena slaves, we spend our time robbing lords. Perhaps *you* should tell *me* what our purpose is, Lio."

"Outlander, you constantly amaze me." Lio leaned forward, clasping his hands together, his brow furrowed by his intensity. "Do you imagine we're going to march into the palace and demand the slaves be freed? What purpose would that serve? We'd be killed or captured, and your friends would still be slaves . . . only we'd be with them. No, Balzan. When we attack the time must be ripe. I'm not a martyr, nor are my friends martyrs. Martyrs don't survive."

"And for you survival is all."

The young Kharnite's face altered; his expression became distant. "No, not all. Not anymore."

"Why, Lio? What's changed?"

"I have, I suppose."

"Oh?"

Lio grinned, exposing his teeth-ridge. "Oh, indeed. You're the one who looks into himself, Balzan. Not me."

74

Balzan decided to change the subject. "I've been thinking about what you said: about the arena, and the huulat slayings, and these yarrotites. There's something I'm not clear about."

"What is it this time?" Lio said wearily. He busied himself putting the coins back into their pouches, and the bags into the sack on the bench beside him.

"What happens to the yarrotites who win?"

"Who win?" Lio's face twisted into a look of confusion. "You mean, who live? The ones who aren't killed in duels?"

Balzan nodded. "Do they come back and fight in the next festival? Or are they freed?"

"Gods, I don't know." Lio sank back, relaxing against the rear wall. His eyes were bright in the lantern light, his face craggy with shadows. "The official word is that they're freed, but I'll be damned if I've ever seen one in the city. But of course, they wouldn't stay in the city, would they? Would you or I?"

"Some would," Balzan said. "At least a few of them would. Are you certain you've never seen a single freed yarrotite?"

Lips pursed thoughtfully, Lio shook his head. "And I've never heard of one returning to his family either, for that matter. It's odd, isn't it? Usually when there's something mysterious like that happening, there are rumors . . . but until you asked just now, I'd never thought about it, never wondered."

"It seems there are quite a few things people don't wonder about," Balzan said. He picked a fowl leg off his plate and bit into it. It was bitter. After a moment of chewing, he said, "Have you ever heard of something called a blood stone?"

"No. Should I?"

"An Alb said something about it before he died. It was in reference to your lords, I think." He took another bite from the leg and tossed the bone back onto his plate, washing the mouthful down with a swallow of wine. "I hadn't given it much thought until now. It's just that things in this city are so strange; the way you Kharnites

75

react—or don't react, rather—to the arena killings, the slums, these lords of yours . . . ."

"Not mine, Balzan."

"The point is, there's something wrong with this city. Whatever it is, it could be connected with these blood-stone things."

"Perhaps. More likely, they're just the mumblings of a rabid barbarian."

Balzan frowned. "I don't think so. He was too serious about it. Apparently something one of Lord Sha's soldiers told him frightened him."

"Knowing what the soldiers say about Sha, he probably used his whip on the savage, or threatened to," Lio said. *"That's* what frightened him." He pushed himself to his feet and lifted the sack onto the table. "Fahl is waiting for us in his shop. We shouldn't keep him waiting *too* long, don't you agree?"

"I'm coming," Balzan said. He wiped his hands on his tunic as he got to his feet and walked behind Lio through the wooden door leading to the front of the tavern. Kharnites shuffled through the murky air, from the bar to their benches. Lio threaded his way past them; Balzan came after.

As he walked, he was thinking and wondering about the blood stones.

2.

The path they took from Fahl's basement shop to the sewer was different from the one Balzan already knew. Lio stepped through a low arch on a street a block from Fahl's, went down a flight of steps between moss-encrusted walls, and came out in a moonlit amphitheater. The amphitheater was enclosed on three sides by high walls which rose into the buildings above; on the fourth side it was bordered by a pool. The water in the pool was layered with scum, and the bushes and flowers set around the pool for decoration were all dead and covered with soot. Beyond the pool there was a garden, also neglected and dead. Balzan stopped at the entrance to the amphitheater and gaped. Lio paused by the poolside, his hands on his hips; he noticed his companion's expression and smiled, with just a trace of wistfullness.

"You see? Parts of Kharn are still beautiful, my friend. Once this entire city was a garden; where we're standing used to be the forum for this neighborhood, a place where people could sing and play instruments, or gather and talk. You could bring your children. Or your lover." The young Kharnite raised his head. "It must have been magnificent."

"Must have been?" Balzan asked. "Was it so long ago?"

"Before my time, at any rate," Lio replied. He sighed and took his hands from his sides. "My father described it to me when he was still alive. We came here when I was a boy, and some of the locals were keeping the garden groomed. I suppose they got discouraged." He snorted. "We're all a little discouraged now."

Balzan started to ask a question—the same question he always asked—but didn't. His footsteps echoed with Lio's as they left the amphitheater and entered a narrow stone tunnel.

"Father told me this led to the community storeroom at one time," Lio explained, ducking under a particularly low stone beam. "Today we use it as an alternate route to the camp, when we're coming from this part of the city."

They collected a torch apiece from a supply kept in a niche, and Balzan struck tinder to light Lio's torch, then his own. Musty smoke curled around them through the tunnel until they came to the remains of a steel-bracketed wooden door, partly rotted away. With Balzan's help, Lio eased the door aside. Balzan heard water dripping in the distance. A shallow ramp dipped away into the darkness ahead of them, sinking from view beyond the light of their torches.

Halfway down the ramp Balzan pulled to a stop, listening. His hand went out and touched Lio's shoulder. The Kharnite started to ask what was wrong; Balzan's fingers tightened their grip, and Lio went silent. They listened.

Far off: a kind of baying.

"No," said Lio softly.

"Quiet."

The baying grew louder, and was joined by another sound: paws padding through water, paws and feet, sloshing threw sewerage and mud.

"They've found us."

"I said be quiet," Balzan whispered. Then: "Who's found us?"

"The soldiers. Can't you hear?"

"We've fought soldiers before. We've the advantage; we know the ground, such as it is."

"You're wrong. *They* have the advantage. Couldn't you hear that baying? They have Stalkers, Balzan. We don't stand a chance."

"Stalkers?"

In the torchglow Lio's eyes were dilated, whether from the darkness or from fear Balzan couldn't tell.

"Huulats," Lio said gently. "Stalkers are huulats, trained to sniff out a man's trail. They'll tear us to pieces."

Balzan swore.

And in the distance, the baying grew ever louder.

Taking a route through the sewer which approached their camp from behind, Balzan and Lio managed to reach the site fully ten minutes before the huulats could arrive. Urro, the heavy-set man Balzan had argued with the first night he spent in camp, was the only rebel awake; the others were roused by Lio as quickly as possible, while Urro and Balzan set about striking the camp. Most of the equipment was personal, to be handled by its owners, but some of the material—such as the large lantern used to light the chamber—belonged to the group as a whole and needed to be disassembled and packed away. Urro had completed his half of the operation when Balzan straightened and said, "We have to give ourselves up."

"Before or after the huulats disembowel us?" Urro asked sardonically. He didn't look up from the pack he was tying.

"I'm serious. We can't make it seem as though we're giving up, of course, but we have to let them take us captive."

This time Urro did glance up, his heavy face frowning. "You *are* serious. You mean it."

"Listen," Balzan said impatiently. "What do they do with captives?"

"If they survive to get captured, they're turned over to the Gamemaster."

"And if they're in good shape physically?"

Urro shrugged. "They're trained to be yarrotites, I suppose. What's the point of this? Have you gone mad?"

"What's wrong?" Lio asked, squatting beside them. "You can't stop packing now; the huulats will be here any moment, and the soldiers behind them."

"He wants us to surrender," Urro said, waving his hands. "You've brought us a fine one, Lio. First he attacks us, now he wants to have us slaughtered." The heavy-faced Kharnite made a disgusted sound and pushed himself erect. He pointed a thick, olive-colored finger at Balzan and said, "You're a fool, outlander. I thought so from the first. You're proving it."

"Balzan, will you tell me what this is all about?"

Balzan blinked from Urro to Lio. "It's what I was saying earlier; all we've done so far is talk. As long as we're outside the palace, we're impotent; we have to get inside those walls somehow, and since a siege is hopeless, as you've pointed out, our only alternative seems to be to let ourselves be captured."

Urro spat. "Let *your*self be captured, outlander. I value my life."

"Wait," Lio said, "wait."

"You wait, boy. I don't have the time." Urro swung his pack onto his shoulder. "Or haven't you noticed? The Stalkers are almost on us."

Lio gave Urro a curt nod, motioning him to silence. He turned back to Balzan, his reptilian features creasing as he made a visible effort to adjust his thoughts. "Balzan, what is it you propose we do? Let the huulats kill us?"

"Never mind," Balzan said. He dropped off the ledge into the sewerage. It went up to his mid-calf, brackish water that left a scummy film on his flesh as it splashed over his legs. He started to unhook the therb from his belt.

He hadn't had cause to use it since he'd entered the city; he'd mostly fought at close quarters, and a therb was useless within a certain distance. "I'll handle this alone. The rest of you can make up your own minds; I've already made up mine."

He cleared his throat, and added quietly, "I'm getting inside the palace—" he flicked the whip out to its full length "—any way I can."

The others—whom Lio had awakened, already on their feet as Balzan finished speaking, their puffy faces brightening as they became more alert—stared at him from the ledge. Urro cursed and hurried away, his bulky figure vanishing into the darkness. Lio stood up, his expression unsure. The Kharnites muttered among themselves; the scene seemed to freeze; and suddenly the tableau was shattered by a baying hiss from the tunnel mouth opposite the campsite ledge.

Balzan turned, and for the first time faced a huulat in the flesh. His stomach knotted; he felt a surge of nausea. He'd thought he knew what to expect, but knowing and experiencing, as he was learning, were two fundamentally different things. He stared at the creature and, unblinkingly, it stared back at him.

The huulat had three heads.

Chapter Nine

Deep within its torso, the huulat reacted to the "sight" of the being before it.

Each of its heads brought the huulat a different view, but two of the views were slightly out of focus, and the huulat's brain concentrated on only one. During a battle all three perspectives would be utilized, as would all three pairs of jaws, and all three sets of teeth, but for simple appraisal only one eye was needed, and the huulat—whose self-concept and nest-name were Hunter-of-Weak-Ones in Balzan's language—customarily sought the view from his central head's orb. The huulat's heads were half the size of a Kharnite's, and flatter, since they contained no brain; Hunter's brain was in its chest, protected by a case of bone and a thick, leathery hide. The huulat was not a very intelligent beast, but it didn't need to be; its instinctive viciousness compensated for its lack of rationality. Hunter was the most deadly predator in its environment, and knew it.

So did its prey. Ordinarily.

But there was something odd about the being facing Hunter across the chamber. There was something in the way it stood, something unnatural in its scent—what the huulat could make out of it, since the chamber was clogged with odors, none of them pleasant to the huulat's delicate nostrils. On each of its heads, Hunter's noses wrinkled with distaste. The effect was both ludicrous and chilling. The huulat sniffed, and blinked each of its cyclopean eyes in turn. All three bloodless eyes stared at the being on the far side of the chamber, watching the being's every move. The huulat waited for a sign of growing panic. None came. The huulat became annoyed.

Beneath the scummy water, Hunter's horned paws shifted to balance its unwieldy weight. Behind it, its tail swept once, twice across the sewerage. And on each head, a mouth opened, displaying a twin array of fierce white teeth.

Its muscles tensed.

The huulat charged.

Balzan didn't wait for the huulat to make its move. When he saw the tendons bunch along the creature's sides, Balzan leaned to one side and whipped his therb forward. The barbed tip shot out and licked the huulat's extreme right head, slicing the skin off the sloping gray brow. The beast didn't seem to notice the attack, however; it plowed forward, spraying muck about its broad shoulders, its heads bending forward as its jaws started to drop open—its three golden eyes gleaming in the light of the smoldering torches on the ledge at Balzan's side.

Balzan spun and dove under the snapping teeth of the left head, splashing through filth as he scrambled to regain his feet. Some of the water got in his mouth. He spat it out, coughing, and turned to meet the huulat's second charge.

It came at once, before he expected.

There was pain in the huulat's eye: bright pain, splitting through his skull. In reflex the huulat blinked its right eye. The pain swelled to bursting—and its right eye went dark.

It was as though a third of the light in the universe had abruptly flashed out. A moment of searing white, an instant of crimson, then . . . nothing.

One of the huulat's eyes was blind.

Hunter-of-Weak-Ones howled and pounded forward. The creature who'd blinded Hunter stood directly ahead. The huulat ducked his heads—the dead one felt odd and unbalanced—and splashed through the fetid water.

Its two remaining eyes were veiled with scarlet rage.

Once more Balzan flicked the therb. This time he missed. The huulat was inside the limit of the therb's effective range; the weapon was next to useless. Realizing this, Balzan tossed the whip to one side, onto the campsite platform where a dozen Kharnites stood gawking, and with his free hand grabbed the hilt of his sword. It was the same blade he'd used against the Albs, the same sword with which he'd gutted the Kharnite soldiers in his tavern room two weeks before. He pulled it from its sheath and hefted its weight. He barely had time to raise it. The huulat ducked under his guard and threw itself against him, and both man and beast went down in a heap, slime gouting around them. Balzan fought back panic and revulsion as the huulat bore him down despite his struggling.

The huulat's second head lunged for Balzan's face.

Balzan jerked his sword around and stabbed.

Scarlet exploded in the huulat's center eye.

The pain was greater than anything Hunter had ever known, a violent force that shoved its way deep into the huulat's brain, burning through every nerve and muscle in the huulat's torso, screaming in every limb, echoing in all of the beast's five senses.

For a moment Hunter-of-Weak-Ones thought it was dead. It couldn't comprehend the pain's intensity; agony filled the huulat's eye to bursting . . . and finally faded.

The huulat forced its last remaining eye to focus on the creature struggling under it. *This* was the creature responsible for *Hunter's* pain. *This* was the creature responsible for Hunter's darkness. Hatred replaced the anger the beast had felt before. Rearing up, it prepared to slash open the creature's vulnerable pink throat. The huulat's jaws opened—

And the most profound pain of all swallowed the huulat, body and soul.

Night washed in from all sides. Hunter-of-Weak-Ones fell forward. Dead.

Balzan heaved the lifeless beast's body off his sword, and using the blade as a cane, hauled himself to a stand-

83

ing position. He looked down at the huulat, lying with its chest gutted by the neutron-sword, the protective bone lying in two sections, the gray matter within the white cup spilling out across the huulat's dead body into the filmy water. The knot in Balzan's stomach broke. He bent forward and retched, his belly heaving. It was the reaction he always had to an animal's death . . . even the death of a beast which had tried to kill him. Only men were responsible for their actions, in Balzan's eyes. All other creatures were helpless. Even the most deadly.

When he looked up, he found himself surrounded by soldiers. The one nearest him was the Kharnite guard whose name was Trull.

Balzan stared at Trull—at his clean new uniform, at the bars marking a promotion, at the dark, hooded eyes—for a full ten seconds.

Then he began to laugh.

2.

The stockade was an open court sixteen levels below the palace arena. At one end of the court there was a railing and some netting, and beyond this a balcony which overlooked the towers of the city. At the opposite end of the court there were crude barracks erected from wood and pig iron which provided cursory shelter from the elements, and little more. Water was available for drinking from two pumps, and for bathing in a central trough; food was brought once, in the morning, and was expected to last the yarrotites until the following dawn. If not for the guards, who were everywhere, and the tower rising behind the court, the overall effect would have been of a poor village on a desert plain. As matters stood, however, the major impression was oppressive, the same sense of oppression Balzan had experienced everywhere in Kharn, concentrated here like some vague supernatural force.

"You're satisfied, I hope," Lio said in a whisper. Squatting next to Balzan, the young Kharnite was surreptitiously testing the strength of his chains. "My friends trusted me, and I'd hate to think I betrayed that trust by convincing them to go along with this scheme of yours."

Balzan gazed at the other Kharnites, clustered around the entrance to the stockade in a desultory group; most of the men he'd met at the underground camp had elected to come along, including, oddly enough, Urro. A few were notably absent, among them the old man who'd interrogated Balzan that first evening two weeks before.

"We'll see," Balzan said. He jerked the chain between his wrists, pulling it taut in unconscious imitation of the young Kharnite beside him. "We have one week until the next festival; time enough to learn what we need to learn and make our plans."

"I certainly hope so," Lio said resignedly.

Balzan noticed a trio of soldiers approaching his group. Leading the two low-grade soldiers was Trull, his face bent in a crooked grin.

"Here's your friend," Urro said. He was sitting on the stone ledge near the entrance, his massive weight looking out of place and awkward at rest. Urro was a man built to move, an animal born for action. He was plainly uncomfortable, and for a moment Balzan felt a great sympathy for the man. The feeling passed quickly, however, and was replaced by brusqueness.

"Quiet," said Balzan. He levered himself to a standing position, using Lio's shoulder; the chains on his ankles made standing difficult.

Trull stopped in front of the group and grinned at Balzan, saying nothing. A bruise over his right eye was beginning to stain blue against his pale green skin. Balzan smiled as he remembered how the Kharnite had received the blow which caused the swelling; it was the result of a reflex on Balzan's part when Trull had grabbed the young man's sword in the sewer, hours earlier. Though Balzan had decided not to resist, his reaction to Trull's abrupt move had been unfortunately beyond his control. He'd swung his fist in a short arc into the Kharnite's face before he could stop himself and had received several blows himself in return. The memory of the incident pleased him.

Balzan was glad Trull bore his mark; it made the capture less of a surrender that way. Unconsciously, Balzan's grin broadened, and Trull's satisfied smirk shifted into a scowl.

"You've nothing to be happy about, outlander."

"That's a matter of opinion, isn't it?"

Trull laughed harshly and waved at the stockade around them. "You're the prisoner. You're the one who'll die in the arena. Or hadn't you considered that possibility, my loose-tongued friend?"

"Here's a possibility for *you* to consider, Trull," Balzan said. "Perhaps I won't die; perhaps I'll be freed. And if I am, *you're* the one who'll be killed. I'll see to it myself."

His features twisting, Trull snarled and backhanded the young human, sending him sprawling at Lio's feet.

A moment passed as the Kharnite soldier stood breathing in short, angry gasps; gradually he drew himself up, made a hacking sound and sent a wad of spittle toward Balzan's feet. The young man jerked his feet away and sat glaring at Trull. The Kharnite chuckled and said, "Even if you do survive the arena, you're no threat to me. The moment you entered this palace, you became a dead man, outlander." Trull's eyes widened, and he added, quietly, "Perhaps from the moment you first entered Kharn."

"So you believe in destiny, do you, Trull?"

Trull noticed the contempt in Balzan's voice, but apparently paid no attention to it. "Not in destiny," the soldier said. "I believe in the blood stones."

Balzan's face went blank. When he spoke, his voice was toneless. "Blood stones?"

"A rumor, outlander," Trull said. "Nothing that need concern you. If you survive the arena, you'll learn the truth of the rumor soon enough." Trull tucked his hands into his belt and turned away. He paused and looked back. "*If* you survive the arena."

The prisoners watched Trull leave. They were silent for several moments after the guards came and released their chains, not one man meeting another's gaze. Balzan sat chafing his wrists; he started when Lio spoke.

"He's heard of them too."

"So it would appear," Balzan replied.

"What *are* these blood stones, Balzan? A headsman's block, do you suppose?"

"Could be." Balzan got up and started across the stockade toward the platform where the food was left in the mornings. Several prisoners hovered around the wood-and-stone table, cutting hunks of near-spoiled meat from the side of a gaapur flank. Balzan approached them, Lio and Urro trailing along with him, and said, "Worry about it after we eat. We can ask the other yarrotites; maybe they've heard something in the time they've been here. *Someone* has to know what a blood stone is."

Though he didn't discover it for another day, Balzan was wrong—no one knew, not even the senior yarrotite, a man who'd been in the stockade for two months, since he was never called for battle during the previous festival —but by the time he learned this, he was caught up in a far more immediate problem.

A problem for which there seemed to be no answer.

3.

He noticed the change in Lio first, though in the beginning he attributed it to nothing more dramatic than depression from being confined. It was only when he tried talking to the other prisoners and noticed that they too were distracted and apathetic, that he began to wonder about the transformation. Lio was acting more and more like a man wandering through a dream. His reflexes slowed, his attention span shortened, he seemed to lose all interest in conversation of any kind—and as the days went by, these symptoms began to appear in the other members of Balzan's group as well. Oddly enough, Balzan himself felt better than ever. Despite the confinement, despite the hours of monotonous training with sword and net—the weapons used by yarrotites dueling in the arena—Balzan found himself reacting with inordinate intensity to everything around him. He was fascinated by the slightest change in his environment: when one of the yarrotites was nicked by accident, Balzan hurried to the man's side and offered his help. The man reacted with confusion; he hadn't yet realized he'd been wounded. Slowly Balzan understood that something was happening to all of them; though he'd changed in a manner opposite to that of his friends, he'd changed . . . and he'd be damned if he could figure out why.

He broached the subject to Lio two nights after their capture. He'd spent the day in the training court with the other yarrotites, exchanging blows, and practicing the subtle twist-throw of the barbed net, but while he'd been training, Balzan had also been thinking, and what he'd been thinking worried him.

Lio, however, wasn't worried. In fact, Lio seemed unbothered by anything. "Changed? I don't think so. Everything seems the same to me. Besides, it doesn't matter. We know what we have to do, don't we?"

He blinked at Balzan with eyes that were strangely out of focus.

"Do we, Lio?" Balzan asked.

"Of course we do."

"Tell me, then. What's our plan?"

"Our plan?" Lio frowned, his features contracting as he concentrated. "To take over the palace, of course."

"How are we going to do that?"

"How?" The young Kharnite waved vaguely. "We'll think of something when the time comes."

"And when is the time coming?"

"Before the festival, naturally." Lio's eyes focused on Balzan. The two of them were sitting in the barrack hut which had been assigned to their group. Lio placed a hand on the young human's chest, the tips of his claws touching Balzan's skin through the cloth of his tunic, sharp and cold against his pale, unscaled skin. "You're too concerned about this, Balzan. Relax."

"I can't relax, Lio. That seems to be the problem." Balzan stared at Lio for several seconds. "I can't relax and you can. Don't you think that's strange?"

Lio shrugged. Balzan gazed at him unblinkingly for several more moments, then got to his feet and walked away.

Balzan was more than worried now. He was terrified.

Chapter Ten

Trito placed his hands on the side of the pool and dragged his dripping bulk onto the glistening tile. He was breathing hard, in short quick gasps, and his face darkened with exertion as he rolled onto his side. Like the others in the vast chamber, he was naked, and when he pushed himself into a sitting position rolls of fat dropped into his lap, his obesity all too visible. Trito was not ashamed of his weight, however; he considered it a token of his success. In a city where most people starved, Gamemaster Trito ate more than well. There were other privileges as well, of course, but those were more subtle and couldn't be flaunted. Perhaps more than the success itself Trito enjoyed the flaunting; to a man who'd struggled up from the depths of a slum, it was life itself.

With a grunt he got to his feet. Whein, his servant, scampered across the tiles, bearing towels and a thick-bristled brush. Trito raised his arms and let himself be dried, idly surveying the other men and women in the communal bath. None of the faces were new to him, of course; in the course of his duties, Trito came to know and deal with most of the nobles and the quasi-nobles of Kharn. Some of the bodies were a surprise, however; he took particular pleasure in studying the sleek figure of a young maiden he'd seen with one of the court noblewomen a few evenings before. The girl had high, round breasts, a well-developed pair of hips, the nub of a prehensile tail, and long, magnificent legs. The maiden felt his eyes on her and glanced in his direction, smiling with recognition; everyone knew the Gamemaster, and the favors he could bestow. Trito leered back. The maiden tossed her head, letting her black hair drift on the water around her shoulders. Trito's leer broadened. She laughed softly, gave him a final demure look, and dove back into the depths of the pool. Trito joggled Whein's shoulder, pointed at the maiden's receding form and said, "Find out her name and invite her to my quarters in an hour's time." Whein nodded and left Trito to complete his drying himself.

There were many advantages to his position, it was true, Trito reflected. Some were more visible than others . . . but others were infinitely more enjoyable.

He received a summons to the chamber of the palace surgeon as he was returning to his apartments. Though he'd had other plans for the afternoon, Trito made arrangements to have them postponed a few hours. He knew the duties of his position as well as he understood the privileges those duties provided. He didn't dare ignore a summons such as this; as Gamemaster he was responsible to the surgeon, and the surgeon was responsible to him.

The surgeon was an old Kharnite, one of the oldest men Trito had ever encountered. At times Trito wondered if the surgeon knew some technique that kept his aged body from dying, some secret which held off the approaching day of death. It certainly seemed so. The surgeon, whose name was Yurl, was so wrinkled, so wizened, he seemed more like a mummy than a living man. Everything about Yurl bespoke age, from the stooped posture to the trembling hands, the quavering voice, the moments of forgetfulness—everything, that is, but for the old man's eyes. They were as brown as Trito's, but there was something about them that made the eyes seem more alive: they were pinpricks glistening in a leathery skull, two dark holes seemingly opened on another universe. Looking at them always brought a shiver to Trito's spine, and so he avoided meeting the old man's gaze as much as possible, even to the point of rudeness. Better to be rude than to feel one's soul sinking into those two dark holes . . . *much* better, as far as Trito was concerned.

"Why didn't you tell me about this new yarrotite trainee?"

91

Yurl asked sharply as Trito entered the surgeon's quarters. The question took Trito by surprise. He stopped in the doorway, puzzled.

"Trainee? Which new trainee?"

"One of my servants overheard a soldier speaking about him," Yurl said. He was seated on a metal bench beside a long examination table, his hands folded neatly in his lap. He wore a gray robe, gray sandals, gray cap. He gave an appearance of calm, but Trito knew from experience that this was only appearance; Yurl was known for his explosive temper. Anxiously, Trito tried to recall anything that could explain what the surgeon was talking about. Something came to him, a report he'd dismissed at the time he heard it, and he said eagerly:

"There *was* a new group of trainees captured a few days ago. I seem to remember hearing something about one of them at the time, but I didn't think . . ."

"You didn't think," the surgeon said flatly. "From what my servant told me, this yarrotite is a freak, a complete anomaly. He may be like nothing we've ever seen before." Yurl unfolded his hands and placed them on his knees, bending forward to peer up at Trito. The Gamemaster looked away from that disconcerting stare. "What do you suggest we do about it, Trito?"

"Shall I have him brought to you?"

"Have him brought to me," Yurl agreed, and added, in a quiet tone that sent a chill through the nerves in Trito's neck, "immediately."

"At once," Trito said, bowing, edging from the room. "At once."

Outside the door, he broke into a waddling run.

2.

"Freak" didn't quite describe the new trainee, Trito decided. There were differences between this yarrotite—called, Trito had learned, Bal-Zan; something like that —and a Kharnite, it was true, but the differences were

92

not so great as those between a Kharnite and, say, an Aeri, one of the winged creatures living on the eastern coast, or between the Queen Myrane and the Red Lord, or . . . Trito searched for another comparison, but could only think of the furred Endorians captured by Sha weeks before. This Bal-Zan was no more a freak than any of these other creatures, Trito thought. He was ulgy, yes, and naked, bald . . . but a freak? Trito thought that was going a bit far.

"Come along," the Gamemaster said. He beckoned across the stockade and the soldiers gripping the young human's arms propelled him forward between them.

Walking with a practiced gait designed to keep his girth from shaking, Trito led the way through the corridors and up the two ramps leading to the level which contained Yurl's quarters and surgery. He listened to the footsteps behind him, and let his mind drift to thoughts of the maiden he'd be meeting as soon as he delivered this Bal-Zan to the palace surgeon. He wondered if Whein had received his instructions and was entertaining the female in Trito's absence. Trito hoped so. He didn't enjoy the chore of making an apology; when he could, he preferred to have his servants perform the task for him. In certain circumstances, of course, that was impractical. Fortunately this wasn't one of *those*.

Entering Yurl's chamber, Trito noticed a curtain at the rear of the room; it moved slightly, as though touched by a breeze from a window beyond—which Trito knew to be impossible. The curtain covered a private passage similar to passages in most quarters, placed for discreet entrances and exits. Suddenly Trito found himself more interested in remaining in Yurl's quarters than in romancing an empty-headed, second-level noblewoman. There was a hint of scandal here, or at least a mystery, and Trito truly *enjoyed* a good mystery, almost as much as he enjoyed a good scandal.

Yurl bustled forward from his examination table, making sounds of approval and interest as he studied the Bal-Zan creature, who gazed back at him with obvious

93

disdain. Yurl walked around the young human twice, then paused and issued a curt order to the soldiers on either side of the young man. Trito watched with amusement as the soldiers stepped forward and gripped the Bal-Zan's tunic. Before the startled youth could do more than cry out, the soldiers tore the clothes from his body. The young man's reaction was sudden, and for Trito, unexpected. Whirling, Bal-Zan kicked his right foot high into the taller soldier's groin, dropped back in time to avoid a slash from the other soldier's quickly drawn sword, then jumped in with a roundhouse blow that caught the sword-wielding soldier over the ear and dropped him instantly. The entire maneuver couldn't have taken more than three seconds, and Trito was still gaping when it was completed. But apparently Yurl had expected something like this, for when the Bal-Zan turned around after dropping both soldiers, Yurl jabbed him in the shoulder with a needle. The young human stiffened; his mouth worked; his eyes widened; he fell. Yurl stepped back to let the Bal-Zan fall past him, smiling as the youth crashed headlong into the near leg of the examination table. Trito swallowed and stared, paralyzed by the sudden violence.

"Help me with him, will you, Trito?"

"What?" Trito forced himself to look up from the young man's sprawled form, and caught himself before he met the surgeon's hard-eyed stare.

"Onto the table," Yurl explained impatiently. He gestured at the soldiers lying near the door, one clutching his groin and moaning. "Neither of them will be of any use for an hour or more, and I'd like to begin on this right away. *If* you don't mind."

Trito shrugged, bent, and with the surgeon's aid, levered the unconscious youth onto the padded table.

"Good. He's quite energetic, don't you think?"

"Very," Trito agreed, wiping the sweat off his forehead and staring at the film it made on his hand.

"More so than the average yarrotite, yes?"

"I suppose so."

"Doesn't that make you wonder, Trito?"

94

The Gamemaster avoided Yurl's steady gaze. "Should it?"

There was a moment of silence. "No," said the surgeon at last. "I would think not. You *are* only the Gamemaster after all. Some things must be kept even from you."

Trito glanced up quickly. "Secrets? There are secrets?"

"It's none of your concern," Yurl said. He pursed his lips and glanced over the body on the table, watching its chest rise and fall, and nodding thoughtfully as he prodded the muscles in the Bal-Zan's neck with his fingertips. "You can go."

"If you don't mind, I'll stay awhile."

Yurl looked at Trito pointedly. "But I do mind, Gamemaster. I said you may leave; leave."

Trito swallowed again, heavily. "You won't injure him? We have a festival inside the week; we need every yarrotite in the stockade."

"I won't harm him," Yurl said. "Now get out."

Stung, Trito backed toward the door. He felt himself flushing a darker green from embarrassment and fear; the embarrassment, because of the way Yurl spoke to him, the utter contempt in the surgeon's voice; the fear, from the look Trito caught when he accidentally glimpsed Yurl's eyes.

Just before he left, Trito cast a final glance into the surgeon's main room. His eyes were drawn past the wizened Yurl, who was bent over the motionless youth on the table, and he looked once again at the curtain in the rear of the chamber. The curtain moved and the Gamemaster caught a momentary view of emerald eyes, pale white skin, ruby-red lips. Then the curtain fell back, the patterns on its silklike material rearranging themselves, but not before Trito was certain of the expression he'd seen on that delicate, noble face. In his years as Gamemaster, Trito had been exposed to most of the more extreme emotions, from the terror visible in a huulat-victim's twisted grimace, to the torment of agony plain on the face of a yarrotite dying beneath a neutron-sword. But until he saw the expression on the face behind the curtain in Yurl's quarters, the face gazing at the naked body of

95

the youth named Bal-Zan, Trito had never seen such a look of soul-consuming, animal *lust*.

It added a whole new dimension to the character of the queen, one which would surely amuse the good Lord Sha.

Chapter Eleven

"What are you?"

Balzan stared. The bent Kharnite leaned his age-creased face closer, his breath sour as he spoke again.

"I asked what you are. You're no Kharnite, no Alb, and not one of these Endorian creatures. On the surface of it, you seem normal enough—apart from the matter of your skin, and this lack of a prehensile tail—but internally, you're completely alien. You have organs I've never seen before, whose purpose I can only guess. So I ask you again . . . what are you, outlander?"

"A man," Balzan said.

For a moment the old Kharnite stared at him, then snorted and turned away. Balzan watched him bend over an array of controls, dials and levers, a few glistening light-plates, some other equipment the youth didn't recognize. When the Kharnite straightened, he was holding a foot-long wand with a spatulate head, in which was set a white crystal. Balzan felt the first real stirrings of alarm. For the past hour, Yurl had examined him with machines vaguely similar to those Balzan had seen in the Teacher's chamber, medical devices with which he'd been familiar: an X-ray machine, a stethoscope, an odd version of an electrocardiogram device, and other probes whose purpose had been clear enough. This wand was new to Balzan, and something in the way Yurl held it told Balzan he wasn't going to enjoy its use. He strained against the force field holding his body on the table, but there was nothing he could do; he couldn't move. He was helpless.

"You have two choices," Yurl said. "You can tell me

what I want to know, where I can find others of your race to experiment with—or you can be dissected. If you're fortunate, I may be able to rebuild you. At any rate, I can assure you you won't die."

"What about the Gamemaster?" Balzan asked. "You told him?"

"I told him what he wanted to hear," the old Kharnite said. "I am the man the Red Lord heeds, not Trito. Have no false hopes on that account, my friend."

"You'll kill me?"

"If necessary."

Balzan scowled. "If I knew where there were others like me, I'd be there with them." He drew in a breath and released it slowly. "In any event, I'd never reveal their location to you. Not even on threat of my life."

"It's not your life I'm threatening, young man." Yurl came closer and pressed the spatulate end of the wand flat against Balzan's naked abdomen. Involuntarily, the young human's stomach flinched, pulling in; the wand pressed down.

"No doubt you've seen our neutron-swords," Yurl said quietly. "This scalpel works on roughly the same principle. With it I can remove layer after layer of skin, without breaking a single blood vessel or completely severing a major nerve. There will be pain, of course—a great deal of pain. I'm afraid it's one of the scalpel's few defects. If I wanted, I could give you a general anesthetic. But then—" and Yurl's face cracked into a grin, the wrinkles around his reptilian mouth sliding into the folds of his cheeks "—there'd be no point to all this, would there?"

"If my hands were free—"

"—you'd kill me," Yurl finished, and nodded. "Precisely why your hands aren't free. But enough of these 'ifs,' Bal-Zan. It's time we dealt with realities, don't you agree?"

Balzan raised his head and spat. The spittle wet the old man's chin and chest. Reflexively, Yurl swung his hand in a backhand blow that whipped the flat end of the wand across Balzan's face. The blow stung, and Balzan was momentarily blinded. When his vision cleared he saw

Yurl glaring at him, the old man's rheumy eyes hard with rage.

"A great deal of pain," Yurl said again.

The wand came down, and scarlet fire burned its way into Balzan's brain.

A moment later there followed darkness, and the deep black well of unconsciousness.

2.

"Hold him up. That's it."

"Is he awake?"

"Just barely. Here, keep his mouth open. Let me give him some water."

Balzan coughed and spluttered as something cool and foul tasting spilled down his throat. He tried to jerk his head away, but calloused hands were gripping his mouth, and all he could do was swallow as much of the tepid water as possible to keep from choking. Gradually he discovered he was enjoying the water, and with this realization came another, and another, and then the memory of Yurl's ancient face leering over him, and the sharper memory of fire burning through his stomach—and suddenly he was awake and totally aware. He shrugged out of the hands of the man bending over him, and opened his eyes. Lio was sitting on a low stool opposite him, and beyond Lio several stockade guards stood watching with casual disinterest, and beyond the guards were the tall iron gates which led to the palace proper. Seeing the gates reminded Balzan once more of what he'd suffered in the palace, and he shook his head for the second time, trying hard to clear it.

"He'll live," a gruff voice said above Balzan. The young human glanced up and saw Urro's tall figure silhouetted against the emerald sky. The bearded man gazed down at Balzan with his one good eye. "More water, outlander?"

Balzan said no, in a voice that even he found barely audible. With an effort, he spoke louder, said, "How long have I been out?"

"Half a day," Lio told him. "At least, that's how long you've been in the stockade. You were gone at least six hours before that. Frankly, we didn't expect you to come back."

"It's strange that you have," Urro added. "And with all your limbs intact."

Startled, Balzan realized this was true. He ran a hand down his chest and over his stomach gingerly. Everything seemed in order—but hadn't Yurl—?

He pushed those thoughts aside. For the time being, he wasn't about to question his good fortune. Whatever had happened in Yurl's chamber, Balzan was certain he'd learn about it in time; until then, he had other, more practical and immediate matters to concern him. Such as . . .

"Food," Balzan said. "Is there any left?"

"Some," said Lio. "Urro and I managed to save some for you. We knew you'd be hungry, if you came to again."

"Optimistic, aren't you?" Balzan said jokingly, as he accepted the handful of meat Lio handed him. The young Kharnite shrugged, his expression dull and listless.

"Just aware of the situation. The odds were you'd never return from your meeting with the palace surgeon; when you did return, the odds were you wouldn't survive."

Balzan frowned. "Didn't you care one way or the other?"

Lio blinked, and said, "Of course. You're my friend, aren't you?"

Taking a bite of the meat—heavy with fat, undercooked and just this side of spoiled—Balzan chewed slowly, thoughtfully, studying Lio's face. The young Kharnite's features were empty of emotion. Looking up, Balzan saw that Urro's face was only slightly more animated than Lio's, the lone good eye still bright, the twisted mouth pulled into a partial frown.

Turning back to Lio, Balzan said, "Of course we're friends," but at the moment, he didn't truly believe it.

Waking the next morning, his first thought was of Kalak, and he remembered that this was a man he'd sworn to kill.

Kalak was the trainer of the yarrotites, a large Kharnite, all knobby muscles and thick, armorlike skin, a towering man of middle years whose brown eyes displayed a look of cruel experience. During the morning and afternoon training sessions, Kalak would swagger through the compound, his neutron-sword swinging at his side, clamped in a heavy fist, his shield over his right arm, his body naked but for a mail loincloth and a glistening sheen of sweat. All of the trainees feared Kalak, and weren't too shy to show this fear. More than once Balzan had seen one of the less agile trainees take a blow from Kalak's sword during lessons, and each time the trainee was killed brutally. Lying awake now in the pre-dawn stillness, Balzan remembered the incident which had occurred the previous day, just before Trito arrived to take the young human to the surgeon's chamber. One young Kharnite who'd befriended Balzan had incurred Kalak's wrath during practice, and the trainer's reaction had been swift and merciless. Kalak had been instructing the yarrotites in the finer points of swordplay, spinning an intricate web of thrusts and arcs through the dusty air with the tip of his blade. The young Kharnite had been watching with full attention as he crossed the stockade toward the group, with word that Balzan was wanted—perhaps too much attention, as it turned out. The boy tripped over a net and stumbled against Kalak, causing the trainer to drop his sword. Before any of the trainees could react, Kalak lunged, grabbed up his blade, spun and cut the edge of the sword through the terrified youth's bare stomach, gutting him. Unbelieving, Balzan watched the young Kharnite sink to his knees, hands clasping his torn belly. Horrified, Balzan saw Kalak step forward, bring his sword back, and slice it through the air once more. There was a spurt of red, a sound like metal slamming wood, and the boy's startled eyes went

101

dull. His head fell at Kalak's feet. The trainees gaped. Balzan became sick. Kalak snorted, releasing his anger.

The next moment Trito arrived and took him away, before Balzan could do more than pull himself erect and take a first hesitant step toward Kalak.

Now, in the dim light filtering through the cracks in the barracks walls, Balzan recalled the scene, and reaffirmed his decision: at the first possible opportunity, he would kill Trainer Kalak. Several things drove him, the day after his interview with Yurl; almost forgotten among his goals was the reason for his being in the place—his desire to free his Endorian tribesmen. Kalak was the more immediate goal; the others would come later, Balzan was sure.

He got off his sleeping mat and moved through the gloom of the long, narrow, one-roomed building which he shared with Lio, Urro, and the others of his "revolutionary" troop. His head throbbed with the last vestiges of the pain he'd suffered at Yurl's hands; he still wasn't fully recovered, though his body was whole enough. Outside the barracks, in the pale green light of dawn, he splashed water from the trough over his face and body, then drank, spitting most of it out after swallowing a mouthful. Straightening, he paused. Across the compound the gates opened and three Kharnite slaves entered the stockade, each bearing a basket of food upon his shoulder. Thoughtful, Balzan watched the slaves dump the food on the block in the center of the compound. There was meat and cheese, and a bland, coarse bread. He waited until the slaves had withdrawn, the gates closing loudly behind them, and then he crossed to the block and picked up a chunk of the sour cheese. He sniffed it. For a moment he stood quite still, his features tightened with anger. Suddenly he hurled the cheese across the stockade, saw it sail out and over the edge of the balcony, and vanish from view beyond. He laughed loud and hard and recrossed the compound to the barracks, ducking through the beads into the darkness.

Kalak was forgotten. His morning hatred was a faded moment in the past.

For the first time since he entered the Red Lord's palace, Balzan knew precisely what he must do.

"Don't eat," Balzan said.

Lio squinted at him in the half-light. The Kharnite massaged his left eye with a hand, looked at the hand, looked at Balzan, and said, "Urro was right. You *are* mad. What do you mean, don't eat?"

"It's the food," Balzan said urgently. He dropped to a squat beside Lio, speaking in a low voice so as not to wake the others in the crowded barracks. "There's some sort of poison, or drug, in the food we've been eating. Possibly I'm immune to it since I'm not a Kharnite, or perhaps it's affected me differently from you, but either way it's dangerous. That has to be the answer, Lio. Nothing else makes sense. Nothing else could explain the way you've all been behaving these past four days."

"How *we've* been behaving?" Lio laughed. "You're the one who's acting insane, outlander."

"You can't be that blind. Haven't you noticed *any* change, in the others, yourself? You're all too apathetic and tolerant. You're all too damned *willing*."

Lio pursed his lips. "There have been a few changes," he said. "That's true."

Balzan grinned triumphantly. "You see?"

"But who's to say they've been important changes? What if a man does become a bit more—well, cooperative?" Lio's eyes shifted as he talked, not meeting Balzan's stare, which was growing more and more alarmed. "Is that such a bad thing?"

"You need to ask?" Balzan said.

Lio seemed uncomfortable. "Even so, what's the point? Why would anyone want to drug us?"

"To get that reaction," Balzan said. "To make us too weak and unconcerned to give them trouble. . . ." His voice trailed off. He realized that Lio wasn't listening, not really. The young Kharnite was already too far gone. "Never mind," Balzan said wearily. "I'll take care of it."

Saying that, he drove his fist in a hard uppercut against Lio's jaw. The Kharnite sprawled back, unconscious.

Balzan got to his feet and looked around. On the far side of the room, Urro was stirring. The bearded man cleared his throat, spat against the wall, muttered something inaudible, finally pushed himself up. When his eye fell on Balzan, Urro groaned and lifted himself to his feet, placing a hand on his back, grunting.

"Lio won't be coming out this morning," Balzan said quietly. Urro glanced at the Kharnite, lying in a heap on his sleeping mat.

"Is he sick?"

Balzan nodded. "A little, nothing serious. But don't bother saving any food for him; he won't be able to eat it."

"The others will be happy to hear that," Urro said. He prodded a man sleeping on the mat next to his. The man woke; soon the rest of the prisoners were getting up, and within minutes the barracks was empty, but for Balzan and Lio. The young human looked down at his companion's bruised face, and listened to the voices of the men in the compound outside, talking among themselves as they bustled around the food block. Their voices seemed dull, their speech mechanical. To Balzan, now aware of the reason for the apathy, it seemed as though the voices belonged to ghosts, shadows of the men he'd known. How many others were drugged like this, apart from the yarrotites? The palace slaves? The soldiers?

The city?

And Balzan understood, at last, the curse which had afflicted the unsuspecting people of Kharn.

Chapter Twelve

The transformation was gradual, but apparent. As the hours passed and morning became midday, and midday dissolved into sweltering afternoon, Lio began to tremble and shake like a man possessed. At first he'd struggled with Balzan—who'd remained in the barracks to ensure Lio's abstinence—but soon he fell into a kind of trance, in which he remained for most of the day. By sunset he was sweating, his body shivering terribly from time to time, his mouth open and drooling, his eyes blank, staring. Balzan watched him twisting and turning on his sleeping mat; after a while Balzan's disgust became pity, and the pity a dull horror. Toward evening Lio's convulsions diminished, and as the night swallowed the last of the daylight, the fevered Kharnite dropped into a full, exhausted sleep.

Leaving the barracks, Balzan realized how sick he felt himself. His stomach was leaden, his neck a knot of muscles, his eyes smoldered like brands in their sockets. He staggered across the compound and collapsed to his knees beside the water trough. The water was cool on his face and hands; he washed himself, and was drinking from the trough when a voice called to him from the opposite end of the stockade.

It was Kalak. The trainer stood near the entrance to the guard's barracks, a building similar in style to those which housed the yarrotites, but more elegantly appointed. Kalak had his hands on his hips, his brown eyes blazing as he studied Balzan with obvious contempt. His sword stood in the ground a few feet from Kalak's right hand.

"You weren't at practice, outlander. Do you know your

sword so well? Or have you so little regard for Kalak that you flaunt your disrespect in his face?"

Balzan rose, painfully aware how naked he felt without his therb. It was gone, lying unused in the armorer's chamber, no doubt. "I meant no disrespect," he said slowly, hating himself for the words. "I was attending to my friend, too ill to care for himself."

"Too ill? Or too frightened of battle?"

"Ill, Trainer. I swear it."

"You swear it," Kalak said, sneering, almost spitting the sentence out. "What's your oath to me, outlander?"

Balzan shrugged. He waited for the explosion of rage he knew would end the confrontation. In a way, he wanted it to happen, and quickly, though he knew it would also mean the end of his hopes of freeing the Endorians. For days he'd allowed himself to be pressured and taunted, however, and he'd about come to the limit of his patience. After sitting through several hours of Lio's torment, sharing his companion's pain vicariously, Balzan had lost almost all his control. Perhaps Kalak would kill him; perhaps he would kill Kalak. Either way, his mission was over. If he survived, he'd be thrown to the huulats for taking the Trainer's life. If he didn't survive . . .

There was no point in considering that.

Kalak took a step forward, his hand reaching out and caressing the hilt of his sword. "I asked, what does your oath mean to me?"

"Whatever you would have it mean, butcher," Balzan said.

With a curse, Kalak jerked the sword from the packed earth of the stockade floor and heaved it over his head, swinging it with one massive hand. Balzan tensed, prepared to lunge out of the way of Kalak's first stroke, knowing that the second blow would almost certainly connect and kill him. The Trainer started to rush forward; Balzan balanced himself on his toes; there was a loud, shrill cry which the young human recognized as Kalak's attack warning—

And an arrow thumped into the ground inches from Balzan's feet, vibrating.

Kalak drew up, startled. Both men turned toward the gate, where the arrow had originated. There, between two husky guards, a young maiden stood, her silk shawl covering her head and pulled under her chin, her eyes watchful and smiling. The guard to her right held a bow and was already stringing a new arrow. Seeing the look on Balzan's face, the female giggled, and the sudden spell was broken.

"So," she said. "Will you kill each other?"

Kalak coughed, glared at Balzan, and said, "I was merely showing the outlander a minor trick of the blade—"

"So I saw," the maiden interrupted. "A more interesting trick would be to see him make use of it once you'd removed his head."

"Milady misjudges me."

"So. You have my apology then."

The tone was mocking, but Kalak bowed anyway. When he straightened, his dark eyes were hooded. "What is it milady wishes?"

"A man," said the maiden.

"I see." The Trainer leered. "Perhaps I can be of service?"

"I think not," the female said disdainfully. "I seek one particular man. He's one of your trainees."

"His name?"

"Bal-Zan." She pronounced it in two separated syllables, as Yurl had, and Trito before him.

From the look on Kalak's face, Balzan was sure the Trainer would fly into a rage. Kalak managed to control himself however, perhaps because a female was present, perhaps for other, subtler reasons. He even performed another perfunctory bow. "The man you seek is here." He gestured at Balzan with the point of his sword. "This is the outlander you call Bal-Zan."

Surprised, the female raised an eyebrow thoughtfully. She stepped back and indicated the open gate. "My mistress requests your presence," said the maiden. "We've already kept her waiting too long. I would advise haste, if you value your strange pink skin."

Balzan crossed the compound, avoiding Kalak's glare,

and as he passed the girl, he asked, "Who is your mistress, milady?"

"You'll see her soon enough."

"Yes, but her name. Whose favor do I enjoy?"

The maiden sniffed. "If she wishes you to know, outlander, she'll tell you herself."

"And if I learn anyway?"

The female grinned, her dark skin lightening. She followed Balzan through the gate, motioned for it to be locked behind them. "Then you'll never leave her chamber alive."

Balzan began to form a retort, thought better of it, and preceded the female up the corridor into the palace proper.

2.

Arches rose into the shadows above, gleaming bands of gold from which hung lanterns of ornate crystal. The room itself was long and narrow, with high glass doors at one end covered by silk curtains, and at the other end, an open balcony. Along each wall stretched a bench of marble, and at intervals along the benches were set small tables of silver. A low couch stood near the balcony, and beside it, a low table, and on the table there was a pitcher and two glasses, and a copper tray holding food. In the air there was a scent of perfume, which grew stronger as Balzan crossed the chamber to the couch. His footsteps echoed on the white marble flooring. His shadow, cast by the light of the various lanterns above, grew and shrank around him as he moved. And though he knew he was alone, having entered the room by himself, and seeing that no one was present, Balzan couldn't shake the feeling he was being observed. He stopped trying. Taking a seat on the couch, he poured some wine from the pitcher, took a slab of meat from the tray, and, eating, waited for something to happen.

For several moments nothing did.

He reclined on the couch and closed his eyes.

Somewhere someone laughed. Balzan didn't react. There

were footsteps, a breath of wind near his face as though a cape had been thrown over a shoulder, and someone sat on the couch beside him. Still Balzan remained unmoving.

"Are you really so unconcerned?" said a voice, soft and feminine.

Balzan looked up. Sitting beside him was a young woman in gossamer, a cape over her shoulder. Her eyes were a bright green, her face was the color of fresh milk, and beneath her almost-transparent gown her body was full and unmarked by scale or fur. She laughed as Balzan surveyed her. Her hand touched his shoulder and her fingers tensed, feeling the swell of his muscle.

"Your name is Bal-Zan, is it not?"

He nodded, saying nothing.

"Do you know who I am, Bal-Zan?"

"I was told not to ask," Balzan replied. "And it's Balzan, not Bal-Zan." At the sound of his voice she smiled.

"And you should not ask," she said. Her green eyes glowed in the slight dimness of the lantern light. "I am your queen. I am Myrane."

Balzan said nothing; waited.

"You're a most frustrating man," the queen said finally. "Any other man of Kharn would be on his knees, but you . . . you simply sit there and stare."

"I'm not a man of Kharn."

"I know," said the queen. She leaned forward, put her hand against his face, and said softly, "What are you then, Balzan?"

"Ask your palace surgeon. *He* should know."

She sat back, her face flushing with anger. "Yurl is a fool. He would've killed you, had I not stopped him. With all his science, he's as ignorant as any petulant child."

"*You* stopped him, milady?" Balzan raised an eyebrow. "Why?"

"Because I saw that you were a man," she said, "and I could not see a man wasted in such a pointless fashion. Are you grateful, Balzan?"

"For my life, yes."

"And will you show your gratitude, Balzan of Endore?"

He started. "You know where I come from?"

"I know many things about you," Myrane said. Her fingers left his cheek and trailed lower. "Would you have me show you?"

He caught her hand and held it tightly. "My queen, a woman with your beauty can have her pick of lovers; why pick me?"

"Because I wanted you. Isn't that enough?"

"And the king—what of him?"

"He's an old fool. I use him as a tool, no more."

"And how does he use you, milady?"

The queen pushed away. When she spoke, her voice had lost its softness, was cold and biting. "The Red Lord uses me not at all, Balzan of Endore. He may think he has power over me, but he does not. He may think I feel gratitude, because he took me as his queen when my own people rebelled against me, but I *do not*. What is between Dragus and me is for our knowledge alone; don't presume to question me, outlander."

"I meant no presumption," Balzan said. He studied the young woman closely, as she studied him. Casually, he asked, "You're not from Kharn, then?"

She laughed, her grim mood broken. "Do I look like a Kharnite sow?"

"Not at all," Balzan admitted.

Myrane nodded, smiling. "I come from a land a great distance from this place, a kingdom ruled by my family for twice a thousand years. I would be there still, but the ungrateful, ignorant beasts turned against their rightful rulers, and I and my mother were cast out, to wander, almost to die, before I came at last to this sad kingdom called Kharn."

"And your mother?"

"Dead," Myrane said, waving the question away with a distracted gesture.

"And so you became the Kharnite queen."

"I was born to rule," she said. "Is it so strange that I should rule here, as my family ruled that other land?"

Balzan shrugged. "And Dragus?"

Myrane frowned. "I told you: the Red Lord is a puppet I use to enforce my will. Do you disbelieve it?"

"No, my queen," Balzan said quickly, though he did, in fact, doubt it quite a bit. Myrane was too young, despite her obvious determination, to so completely influence a man like the Red Lord—about whom Balzan had heard a great deal, none of it spoken with good will. "As you've said before," Balzan continued, "I'm a stranger to this land. Much of what is familiar to you is utter confusion to me."

"Most of life is a mystery, Balzan," said the queen. She came forward and put her lips against his. "The wise man admits it, and seeks only to survive and enjoy." She kissed him, then slowly drew back. "The fool tries to learn that which he can never know, and so wastes the precious hours of life, to no purpose."

"Perhaps, milady."

"You doubt it?"

Balzan spread his hands. "I don't know one way or the other. I merely hope that survival alone isn't all a man can strive for."

The queen's face darkened. "There are other things as important as survival," she said. Opening her gown, she came close to him again, pressing her flesh against his; he sensed the heavy sweetness of her perfume, the warm breath against his neck as she spoke. "If you're strong enough to take them," she said.

Again she kissed him. The kiss lengthened, and for a moment Balzan began to respond, but only for a moment. Sensing some change in him, the queen broke away suddenly and stared wordlessly into his eyes. Balzan felt himself being probed in some uncanny way, felt the deepest secrets of his mind and body being drawn from him, swallowed by those fathomless emerald eyes, but even so he couldn't tear himself away from her gaze. In the distance an animal cried out, its calling echoing from tower to tower across the city like a ghost's wail. When the cry faded, Myrane shivered, dropped her stare and said, in a voice thick with rage, "Get out of here. Get out, before I have your pale pink body torn and tossed to the blood stones. *Get out.*"

Knowing she'd somehow seen his true feelings, his feeling of disgust and repulsion, and knowing that to remain would be a pointless risking of his life, Balzan left the chamber without a backward glance.

And behind him the queen sat very still, as still as a statue, save for her hands, which trembled in her lap as she tightened them together into gnarled and mottled fists.

3.

He said nothing to the guards who met him outside the queen's chamber, and they said nothing to him. Silently the three of them went back down the passage Balzan had taken in the opposite direction only a half hour before. There were light plates set into the ceiling every twenty paces, and occasionally a window broke the gray wall to their left; but apart from these few tokens to lighting, the corridor was as dark as any pit. For this reason, and also because he was lost in his own thoughts, Balzan didn't see the slim figure walking toward him until he collided with her. The tray the servant girl had been carrying clattered loudly to the floor, spilling its contents over the stones, a cup bouncing to a stop near Balzan's bare foot. He picked it up and held it out to the girl, and started to apologize, but froze in mid-sentence. The girl stared at him, her eyes widening, the golden fur of her face rippling as she smiled, her eyes suddenly full with tears—and then she was in his arms, sobbing over his chest, and he clutched her tightly, ignoring the muttered protests of the two guards.

"Kitta," he said at last. "Kitta, are you all right? They haven't injured you, have they?"

Before the Endorian female could answer, a meaty hand clapped her on her shoulder and jerked her away.

"No talking," the guard said, his reptilian face twitching into a cruel grin. He started to say something else, but never finished. Balzan's bare foot came up in a sharp kick that connected with the Kharnite's throat just below the

112

chin. There was a sharp, splintering crack, and the guard flipped over backward into the passage wall. His skull struck the wall with a hard wet sound. Before the first guard had slid to a half-sitting position against the stone floor, his glazed eyes staring unseeingly into the shadows further along the corridor, Balzan had already turned on the second.

The second guard was a large Kharnite, long and bony, with pop eyes that gaped like red mouths as Balzan kicked his partner. This guard's reflexes were better than the other's, however; even as Balzan danced back from the first, falling soldier, the second Kharnite had whipped his blade free from his scabbard, and was lunging it toward the young human's unprotected belly. If the thrust had connected, Balzan's gut would have been sheared open just like the young Kharnite who'd crossed Trainer Kalak; naturally, the thrust missed.

Two seconds later the Kharnite was dead, his neck bent back at an impossible angle, his long reptilian tongue protruding from between dead lips, his eyes as empty of life as his former companion's.

Kitta had observed all of this with horror. As Balzan straightened from the second guard, whose neck he'd snapped, she rushed toward him, crying. He embraced her briefly, then stepped back, his face intent as he listened to the sounds around them.

"No one's coming," he said, "but someone will be along any minute. Is there someplace we can go, where we can talk?"

Kitta started to shake her head, stopped, and said, "Lord Sha's chamber. No one's there at this time of day."

Balzan let himself be led down a side passage into a wide room with a claustrophobically low ceiling. There was a carpet on the floor, a dark maroon, and furs and hides on the walls. Beside the window there was a sunken area filled with pillows of various sizes and shapes, made from different kinds of cloth and hide. Kitta led him to this, moving with a frightened air, settling herself nervously on a square pillow opposite him. Her hand was still in

113

his, and Balzan noticed that her fingers were trembling and cold.

"This is milord's bedchamber," Kitta explained. "If he finds us here, he'll kill us both."

"You mean Lord Sha?"

Haltingly, Kitta told Balzan what had happened to her the first day in Kharn, how she'd been picked to be one of Lord Sha's servants, how she'd had trouble with the woman Scala, and how Sha had taken her under his personal care. When she finished, she added, "He's been good to me, my brother. He hasn't mistreated me, he's been very kind to me. . . ."

"But you're his slave," Balzan said quietly.

"It's not so bad."

"Not so bad?" He shook his head. "Being another man's property?"

"Don't you see? It's the way things are. What can I do about it?"

"Have you tried to escape?" Balzan cast a look toward the door they'd closed behind them. Outside, there was a sudden cry. "They've found our friends," Balzan said. "They'll be after us soon." He turned back to Kitta. "Well?"

"I don't understand what you mean by escape."

"Kitta, you're someone's prisoner. You're not free. Don't you want to be free?"

"Of course," Kitta said, "but I'm not."

"Yes, that's the point."

"What's the point?" Kitta's voice broke. "Balzan, you're confusing me. If I'm a prisoner, then I can't be free. It's not for me to decide; it's for Lord Sha."

Balzan dropped his hands from her shoulders wearily. She was reacting the same way Lomar had, as any Endorian would. To one of the Cat People, the concept of free will, of changing the direction of one's own life, was totally alien. They accepted. No matter what happened, they accepted. An Endorian might fight to stay alive, but he'd never fight to change the way he lived. It wasn't part of his nature.

If Kitta or any of the other Endorians captured by the

114

Kharnites were to be freed, it would be up to Balzan to free them, if he could. This was something he'd always understood, yet even so, it annoyed him.

There was a yell outside the chamber, the pounding of booted feet.

Balzan glanced over his shoulder at the doors, then back at Kitta. "Never mind all that," he said. "Will you be at the festival?"

"I have to be. I go with Lord Sha."

"Fine. I'll see you there."

"Balzan," she said, taking his arm as he started to rise. The shouting was louder now. Doors opened and slammed in the corridor beyond Sha's chamber as the guards carried their search down this side hall. "Why are you here?" Kitta asked. "You weren't one of those captured . . . I don't understand how—?"

"I'm a yarrotite," Balzan said. "I'll be fighting in the arena. For now, that's all you have to know."

"A yarrotite? But that means . . ." She began to cry again. "You'll be killed."

"Not necessarily," Balzan said. He turned and started across the chamber.

He'd almost reached the doors before they burst open and the guards swarmed in around him.

Chapter Thirteen

Lord Sha brought his whip up and slashed down in a single continuous motion that was as graceful as it was merciless. Across the clearing, a slave cried out and twisted in agony against the scarred wooden punishment post, back arching. The other slaves of Sha's retinue, standing in a half-circle around the post, winced as the barbed tip of the whip sliced a green line down the slave's back. They glanced at each other, at the slave being punished, and at Sha, who noted their terrified response with satisfaction.

He waited a moment, then used the whip again.

This time the slave's groan was barely audible. The slave slumped against the post, apparently unconscious, his long body limp, his reptilian tail twitching spasmodically in the dust. He was an Alb—one of the few Albs brought back from Sha's last expedition. Like the others he'd quickly spent the money he'd been paid for helping with the herding of the Endorian prisoners, and like the others he'd been thrown into prison when his money ran out. Again, like the others, he'd become a slave. He'd been a problem since the first—he couldn't seem to accept the change in status, or understand its full meaning—and at last it'd become necessary to discipline him, a chore Lord Sha ordinarily neither relished nor performed with real energy. Today, however, it was different. Today he'd applied himself to the task with enthusiasm, enjoying the gradual disintegration of the Alb's physical strength, wallowing in the destruction of the slave's identity and will. It had released the tensions building within him since his last meeting with Trito the day before, though not completely.

To completely release his tensions, Lord Sha would have had to kill—and this was a luxury he was not willing to permit himself. Not yet.

"Untie him," he said to the slaves nearest the post. "Give him some water, take him back to the palace and find him a physician. I want him on his feet by the festival." The slaves hurried to comply. Sha turned on his heel and strode across the clearing into the wood beyond.

Walking along the familiar path which led to the river he'd known since childhood, Sha forced himself to relax. Slowly, the muscles in his face relaxed, and his expression eased from a scowl to a look of restrained rage. He concentrated his attention on the sights and sounds and smells around him, seeking to distract himself from what Trito had told him on the previous day. To the south rose the towers of Kharn, shining in the noon sun, bright and dreamlike through a veil of leaves. To the west were mountains, blue-tipped peaks thrusting into the pale green sky, harsh and cold . . . no more cold, Sha thought grimly, than the anger within him.

Even as this thought came, he pushed it away. He studied the flowers bordering the path. Red and green and yellow and purple, they spotted the pathway with color. Large blossoms, small; long stems, short; there were a thousand varieties, each different, all beautiful, some deadly. He saw the bright scarlet globe of a jaffa plant, a seemingly harmless weed whose pollen caused a rash which ultimately poisoned the entire body if not treated properly and quickly. Seeing the jaffa, Lord Sha smiled. It was a day when deadly things amused him. He lifted his head and scented the air, sweet with the perfume of a dozen deadly blossoms. . . . For a moment he toyed with this idea, then, like the earlier thought, banished it from his mind. He walked on, and came at last to the river.

Here the banks were swollen with the seasonal flood. Normally the waters moved strongly over the rocky riverbed, but now they were a torrent, tumbling wildly away in swirls and eddies around the larger stones and boulders, churning against the muddy shores. Sha stopped on a grassy rise overlooking the river and stared into its depths. He didn't hear the footsteps approaching. He looked up, startled, when Trito touched his arm. The Gamemaster stepped back at Sha's scowl and jerked his hands together nervously.

"Don't ever touch me like that, Trito."

"My apologies, my lord. I didn't realize—"

Sha gave a curt gesture and Trito went silent.

"I've been considering what you told me," Sha said softly, staring into the waters at his feet, "and I've decided that you're either mad or a traitor." He brought his eyes up from the river and gazed at Trito coldly. "Either way, you obviously deserve to die."

The Gamemaster's mouth worked anxiously. "My lord, I—I don't know what to say. Yesterday you—"

"Yesterday was yesterday, Trito. I believed your lies yesterday. I do not believe your lies today."

"But, milord—"

"*Quiet!*" Sha glared at the quivering Gamemaster, who subsided, but still stared at Sha with wide, panicky eyes. "I've listened to as much of your whimpering as I care to. You told me yesterday that the queen expressed desire for a slave . . . a yarrotite. This lie alone would be enough to ensure your end. But to claim that this yarrotite was a freak, not even a *man*. . . ."

Sha paused, and said coldly, "A lie such as that will earn you a painful death indeed."

"It's not a lie, milord," Trito cried. "I can prove every word."

"How?" Sha asked, sneering. "You said yourself that you were alone, that Yurl and this freakish yarrotite were the only others present. Will you change your story to suit your convenience? Do you want to compound your falsehood, Trito?"

"No, my lord," Trito stammered. "I have new information. . . ."

"Oh? That contradicts this treacherous lie?"

"On the contrary," the Gamemaster said hurriedly, "It confirms it."

Darkening, Sha took a step forward. His hand swept

118

out, smashed backhand across Trito's face. Sha began to unsheath his sword as Trito raised his hands reflexively. "I can prove it, Lord Sha," the Gamemaster said. "There were witnesses—the queen's own slave—"

Sha let the sword slide back into its sheath. "Witnesses?"

"Aye, milord."

"And where are the witnesses?"

"The girl is here," Trito said. "I took the liberty—"

Sha broke in. "Here? You brought a slave *here?* By what right? I swear, Trito, a traitor's death is too easy for you. . . ."

"Please, my lord," Trito said quickly. "I knew you would want to speak with this girl, to question her. It was merely my intention to hasten the matter. My lord, I meant no offense."

Gradually Sha's expression softened. Almost wearily, he waved a hand past his face, as though to brush away the exhaustion plainly visible there.

"You're forgiven, Trito. I never told you I considered this a private place. You did no wrong." Sha sighed. "In fact, if this story of yours is true, you've done me a great service. A bitter service, perhaps, but no less because of that."

Trito's face went blank. In a toneless voice that did much to conceal his exultation, he said, "My Lord Sha is too kind. I've only done what I consider to be my duty. Would you see the girl now?"

Sha nodded. "Bring her out."

Grinning to himself, Trito hurried back down the path from the river. It was all developing precisely as he'd hoped. There would be a great deal of trouble, he was sure, but it little concerned him. In the end, he, Trito, would benefit; of that he was certain. Nothing else worried him.

Nothing else could.

2.

Kitta was in the slave's kitchen when Lord Sha returned from the field. She'd been helping the cook prepare a special meal, one of Sha's favorites, and she looked up with surprise at the sounds of commotion coming from the hall. The cook, an elderly Kharnite female who'd been beaten too often and too brutally and was somewhat the less intelligent because of it, began to whimper as the voices in the hall grew louder. Kitta glanced at her, concerned, and looked toward the doorway, then back at the old woman, who stood trembling over the hip-high stove.

"What is it? What are you afraid of?" Kitta asked.

The old woman made a hushing gesture. "You don't want him to hear you—not now, not when he's like this."

"You mean Lord Sha?"

The cook's eyes widened. "Don't you hear them? He's in a rage. Someone's going to die today, I promise you."

"But why?" Kitta turned toward the archway, where the sounds seemed to be heading. "Lord Sha's always been so kind. I can't believe—"

"Believe what you will—look!"

Kitta gaped as a group of ten male slaves entered the kitchen, bearing a limp, bleeding Alb on their shoulders. As she watched, bewildered, they set the Alb on the long, low table used to prepare food for cooking. The men milled around, their eyes rolling, mouths working as they whispered among themselves. Kitta stared at the injured man. She was horrified. The man's back was a torn, bloody mess, green ichor spreading and seeping from a dozen lashes, staining the wooden table, spilling onto the stone floor. Beside her, the cook moaned and swooned. The Endorian managed to catch the old female before she collapsed; she was startled to find the woman so light.

One of the men broke from the group and helped Kitta ease the cook to the ground. When the two of them straightened, the slave gave Kitta a searching look and asked, "Are you the cook? Can you help us?"

Kitta shook her head no, but at the man's despairing look, said, "What do you want me to do?"

"M'lord told us to find a physician," the slave explained. "Drui will die if he isn't bandaged, and we don't dare go to one of the palace surgeons. They'd as soon kill him as save him. And m'lord would be angered if the Alb died." The man shivered. "And milord is a villain when he's angered."

"You need bandages?"

"You see how he is," the Kharnite slave said, waving a hand at the bleeding Alb. "Someone has to stop the bleeding. We thought the cook—" He let his hand drop to his side and started to turn away.

"Wait," Kitta said. She swung around, pointed at an apron lying on a counter. "Tear that cloth into strips. I'll see what I can do."

The relief on the man's face was almost pitiful. Kitta was shocked by the depth of emotion the Kharnite displayed. Somehow it frightened her more than Scala's unrestrained viciousness had—what it implied, the force which had been used to inspire such terror, was more horrifying than the worst fate Scala could impose. Stilling a rising nausea, Kitta moved nervously across the room to the bleeding Alb's side.

She would do what she could to help him.

An hour later, Kitta left the passage outside Sha's private chamber and entered the room adjoining it. The guard standing before Sha's door gave her a friendly smile, which she returned. Otherwise, he ignored her; she was a familiar face around the lord's rooms.

Closing the door of the antechamber behind her, Kitta leaned back against the jamb, shut her eyes, and forced herself to relax. Her heart, she found, throbbed painfully in her chest. She hadn't realized how afraid she was, how worried she'd been that the guard would stop her, question her for some reason, perhaps even send her before Sha. And after what she'd been told by the slaves about Sha's behavior that afternoon, an audience with her lord was the last thing Kitta desired.

Opening her eyes, she surveyed the room she was in. It was a small parlor, used primarily for receiving formal guests. Along one wall a window revealed the city and distant hills; along another a counter stretched, polished marble and glass, where food would be served during a reception. There were chairs in the room, small tables of wood, a couch of plush velvet. And in the wall adjacent to the window, there was a locked door framed by two red-velvet curtains. It was this door Kitta now approached, moving as silently as only an Endorian could. She'd removed her shoes as soon as she'd entered the room. Now she walked on her bare feet across the cold marble floor soundlessly, the pads beneath her toes cushioning each step. Deliberately, she hadn't lit a lantern; the room was pitch-black; she was a shadow in the darkness.

She reached the door, pressed up against it and put her eye to the slit where the door touched the jamb. By squinting, she could make out a figure standing in the next room, gesticulating angrily. It was Lord Sha—a Sha she'd never seen before—his features dark with rage, his eyes an angry yellow, the tendons in his neck bulging as he ranted. She couldn't see the person he was talking to; all she was able to make out was Sha and part of the room behind him, and the table at his side. Watching, she saw Sha pick up a goblet from the table, break off his speech, and down the goblet's contents in a gulp. Another voice spoke then, a thick indolent voice Kitta recognized as belonging to Gamemaster Trito, a man she'd seen often in the past few days in Sha's presence. She put her ear to the crack and listened. After a moment she could understand what the two men were saying, and listening, she became more and more horrified.

"I want him finished."

"But, my lord—the Games—"

"Never mind the Games, Trito. I don't care how you arrange it; that's your concern. If you care for that stretched hide of yours, you'll see it done. And at once."

Kitta put her hands against the door and shifted her weight, changing her angle and putting her eye—her left one this time—to the slit again. She could now see Trito sitting on the edge of a small stool. Even in his tailored robes, the Gamemaster was bulky and immense, a mound of obesity. He was sweating now, using the sleeve of his silk tunic to mop the moisture from his sloping brow.

122

"Of course. Of course. If that's what my Lord Sha wishes—"

"It's what I wish." Sha strode into view, swung around Trito's chair, and disappeared again. His voice remained strong, however, and Kitta had no difficulty understanding his words. "You must realize, Trito, it's not what you think. Not a matter of injured pride. The queen is free to pick her lovers; who am I to deny her that privilege? No. It's a matter of decorum. She may love whomever she pleases, but if that lover is a slave—well, you can see it just wouldn't do for him to remain alive to advertise the queen's indiscretion, now would it?"

"No, milord," Trito said anxiously. "It wouldn't do at all."

"You *do* understand then. Good." Coming back into view, Sha stopped momentarily behind Trito's chair and stared over the Gamemaster's head, his expression distracted.

"Tell me, Trito," he said finally, "how will you have it done?"

"Perhaps an accident," Trito answered. "The queen would be displeased if she thought we'd interfered."

"Quite right," Sha murmured.

Trito looked thoughtful. He brightened. "Kalak," he whispered.

"What's that?"

"Kalak, milord. The Trainer."

Sha's furrowed brow smoothed. "I've heard of him. He's insane, isn't he? And powerful, from what I've been told."

"Very powerful, indeed, milord."

Sha nodded slowly. "A fight, perhaps?"

"It can be arranged." Trito lifted his massive shoulders in a lazy shrug. "According to my information, he and this Bal-Zan have already become entangled."

"Excellent," said Sha. "See to it, Trito. You'll be well rewarded, naturally," the lord added as Trito rose. The Gamemaster made a deep bow, as low as his ample stomach allowed.

"My lord is too kind."

"Nonsense," Sha replied. He clapped a hand on Trito's

arm and led him out of Kitta's view. She heard their voices continue after they'd passed from sight, but she missed what they said. She'd missed most of the last exchange between the two Kharnites; for several seconds, all she'd heard were the mental echoes of the name Trito had spoken, a name she knew as well as she knew her own: *Balzan*. They'd been discussing Balzan; they'd arranged his death as one would arrange a dinner engagement. Gradually the shock left her and she wakened to the fact that she'd been standing motionless, paralyzed, at the door for almost a full minute. There were no voices in the other room now. Both men had left. She was alone.

Almost stumbling, she crossed the room to her shoes, put them on and left. The guard in front of Sha's door grinned at her as she passed and frowned when she didn't return the smile. She never noticed.

3.

Scala touched Fayra's arm, and with her other hand pointed at the slim figure hurrying toward them down the narrow hall leading to the main palace corridor. Fayra clacked her jaws together; Scala leered. The two of them stepped in front of the female as she turned the slight bend in the corridor which had concealed them from her. She jerked to a stop, staring at them, first without comprehension, then with apparent horror. Scala folded her arms, leaned back her pink head and laughed—a throaty laugh that obviously frightened the slender Endorian, because the girl's yellow fur flattened on her face, and her color went from a light tan to an ashen gray.

"We've kept our eyes open for you," Scala said. Her voice was low and husky. "You're a sly one, aren't you?"

"Please, let me pass." The young female's words were scarcely loud enough for the two older women to hear. "I have to deliver a message. It's very important."

"Possibly," said Scala, glancing at Fayra in amusement, "but it'll have to wait. We simply *must* have our talk first. You remember our talk? We were going to have one the

124

the other evening, before you were called away. Isn't that right, Fayra?"

The reptilian female clacked her jaws, her lipless mouth stretching into a skeletal grin.

The Endorian female looked from one to the other. There was an emotion visible in her eyes that wasn't quite terror, but rather more a kind of terrified despair. In an almost mechanical reflex, she began to scream as the two older females closed in.

This time there was no one to hear.

Chapter Fourteen

"You understand what we want? Completely?"

"Perfectly. There'll be no difficulty." The Trainer's bony cheeks seemed to crinkle as he smiled. "I promise."

"See that there isn't," the Gamemaster said sardonically. "If this succeeds, it could mean your freedom, come the Games three days from now."

Kalak started to express his thanks, but before he could begin, he was stopped by Trito's weary hand. The shadow of the hand loomed large on the barracks wall, cast by the fire in the compact metal stove before which the two Kharnites sat. "Don't bother," Trito said. "Just do as I've asked. That'll be gratitude enough."

He preceded the Trainer out of the hut. The sun was setting, and the horizon was a mingling of colors, hot and cold.

"You'll do it tonight?" Trito asked.

Behind him, Kalak nodded. "Within the hour."

"Remember," the Gamemaster said, tugging his cape around his shoulders to ward off the evening chill. "Make sure—quite sure—he's dead.

Bowing, Kalak broke into a grin.

2.

Lio finished vomiting, wiped a hand over his mouth, studied his palm with distaste, and at last turned his attention to Balzan, squatting beside him at the water trough.

126

"It still hits me now and then. You're sure it's drugs?"

"That seems like the only answer," Balzan replied.

Lio shook his head. He examined his reflection in the drinking water of the trough critically. His face was haggard and drawn, his brown eyes tinted slightly yellow, his normal green complexion a shade lighter, his hair ragged and unkempt. "I fell for it completely, didn't I?"

"Everyone did, Lio."

"Not you," the young Kharnite pointed out dryly.

"Do I have to keep explaining? I'm not like you, Lio. Whatever was in that drug—in the food they fed us or the water we drank—made you passive and me hyperactive." He held out his hand. It trembled slightly. "My nerves are so sharp that I haven't slept well all week."

"I notice you're still eating and drinking, though."

Balzan blinked at the handful of meat on the tray in his lap. He shrugged. "Sharpened reflexes don't strike me as a detriment, Lio. There's no point in starving myself if these drugs aren't doing me real harm."

"How do you know they're not?"

Balzan grinned. "I don't. It's just that I'm not really worried."

The Kharnite sat back on his haunches. He took a glance over his shoulder, at the hut behind them. Through the half-open curtain, Urro could be seen sprawled unconscious on a sleeping mat. "You think it's over for him now?"

"Probably. He looks about like you did last night, after you'd finished getting the drug out of your system."

Lio rubbed the back of his neck ruefully. "I'll bet I didn't give you half as much trouble as he gave us. I'd swear he'd broken my neck, the last time we had to hold him down."

Balzan said nothing; he took a bite of his meat and chewed it thoughtfully, unaware of the look Lio was giving him.

"What do we do now?" Lio asked, breaking the silence. "Raid the guard barracks and take over the palace?"

"That's hardly practical."

"I wasn't serious." Lio traced a pattern in the earth

near his thigh. "We have three days, Balzan. Three days, and then we have to fight in the Games. So far it's just you, Urro, and I. What can we do against the entire Kharnite army?"

The young human raised an eyebrow. He turned his gaze on the setting sun.

"We'll think of something," he said.

3.

The sound came again: a soft whisper of cloth on sand, the dry rasp of hushed breathing. Balzan remained motionless on his sleeping mat, lying on his side with one arm cushioning his head, his free hand on the small knife near his middle. He'd had the knife from the beginning of his time in the stockade, having pilfered it from the armory during the first day of training, and he'd kept it with him always since then, even while sleeping. It was about the size of an Endorian hunting knife, but with a serrated blade that would make an ugly wound entering an opponent's body, and an uglier wound withdrawing. Touching the blade, feeling its sharp outline, Balzan was vaguely reassured, but even so he didn't let down his guard for an instant. It was good that he didn't; the moment after he'd come awake after hearing the alien sound in the barracks, he stiffened at the crunch of footsteps near his head and whirled in time to avoid the sudden slash of neutron-sword. The blade whistled as it passed within inches of his skull. It thumped into the ground, slicing neatly through the top of Balzan's sleeping mat, passing almost half a foot into the packed earth flooring before his attacker brought it up short. Balzan rolled to his feet and stared at the husky silhouette confronting him. Kalak grinned back, his jaws catching a ray of moonlight from the open doorway, flashing like teeth in the darkness.

"You tried to kill me," Balzan said softly, wonderingly. The Trainer laughed, a dry cough that chilled the young human when he heard it.

"Not as stupid as you seem, are you? With a little practice, you might develop the brains of a gaapur."

Kalak noticed the knife in Balzan's hand and laughed harder. "Though if you try to use that little sticker on me, you'll never have the chance, I promise you."

Balzan hefted the knife, eyed the sword in the other man's hand, and waited, wordlessly.

"We argued earlier," Kalak said. "We were unable to finish our argument. Perhaps we can finish it this evening?" He spoke slowly and formally, in the style Balzan had come to know Kharnites to use when making a challenge.

"If that's what you want," Balzan said.

"Ten minutes," the Trainer replied. "In the practice area."

"I'll be there."

"See that you are."

With that, Kalak quit the hut, dropping the curtain into place behind him. Balzan let out a breath he hadn't been fully aware of holding, and glanced at the knife in his hand. It seemed pitifully small now, though it had felt large enough when he'd confronted Kalak. For a moment he wondered why the Trainer had chosen this night for a formal challenge, and then he dismissed the thought: it didn't make any difference, not really. It would have happened sooner or later, and in a way Balzan was glad it was happening now; it would be one less problem he'd have to deal with the following morning.

Assuming there would be a following morning, of course.

He'd collected his clothes and was almost fully dressed when a voice said, "You're not really going, are you?"

Balzan looked around at Lio, who sat with his legs drawn up under his chin, his blanket in a heap at his feet. "I don't have a choice," Balzan said. "You saw what happened?"

"Just the last part of it."

Balzan described Kalak's attempt on his life. When he was done, he noticed that Lio's face had gone pale, or as pale as a Kharnite's face *could* go. The young Kharnite made a hissing sound between the ridges of his teeth, shook his head in dismay. "I see what you mean. You *don't* have a choice."

"No," Balzan said, slipping his tunic over his head and straightening it around his waist. "And that's just the way Kalak wants it. I don't have a choice at all."

Only one moon was up, casting a diluted glow over the city of Kharn, the diminished light giving the shadows a ghostly appearance, somewhat blurred and ill-defined. Objects which would have been completely visible earlier in the evening were now indistinct. Distances were confusing. A light mist rolled across the stockade, muffling sound. Nothing seemed to have its proper visual weight; nothing sounded right. Inwardly, Balzan cursed his luck; on a night like this, battle with Kalak would be doubly dangerous. Fortunately, Kalak would have the same difficulties as Balzan, but Kalak was the more accomplished in-fighter; the loss of full moonlight could give him an added advantage over his human opponent . . . as though the Trainer needed an edge. Kalak was the deadliest man Balzan had ever encountered, as well as the most vicious. Balzan knew he could expect no quarter, no mercy, no accidental slip; he was in for the fight of his life. And, possibly, the last.

As he crossed the stockade, he did his best to conceal his feelings. He tried to appear confident, almost cocky, in an effort to make Kalak underestimate him. It was a futile effort, he knew; if anyone in Kharn was aware of Balzan's abilities as a fighter, it was Kalak. The Trainer had observed him practicing with sword and net for a week. Still, there was always the chance that Kalak's monumental ego would betray him. It was a chance Balzan intended to utilize completely.

Beside Balzan, Lio walked nervously, casting apprehensive glances at his companion, as well as at the Kharnites they approached. Lio was dressed like Balzan in light fighting gear—loose tunic, leggings, sandals strapped to the knee, a band of leather holding his hair from his eyes. Theoretically he was Balzan's second. In point of fact, he was there for moral support alone, to try to see that Kalak

130

kept foul play to a minimum. To try, only. If Kalak decided to ignore the rules of combat, there was little Lio could do, and all concerned knew it. Especially Lio. Judging by the miserable expression on his friend's face, Balzan could see Lio wasn't happy about the situation. Neither, for that matter, was he.

Kalak, however, was positively ecstatic. He stood at the edge of the practicing rink, his fists on his hips, grinning as he watched Lio and Balzan come toward him. His body was covered with a sheen of perspiration, his scaly skin slick with sweat. He was wearing only a loincloth of mail and a belt holding his scabbard and sword. His bald head was naked, shining in the moonlight. Beneath his scaly skin, his muscles rippled when he shifted position and stepped back to allow Balzan and Lio inside the circular area. Lio noted despairingly that Kalak was almost a full head taller than Balzan, as well as broader across the shoulders and chest. Next to Kalak, Balzan was a runt. Lio shook his head sadly, unable to meet his friend's eye.

"Weapons are by the wash-trough," Kalak said tightly. "Pick one. We'll start immediately."

Balzan chose a neutron-sword, ignoring the belt and sheath, hefting the weapon appraisingly and cutting it in a few brief strokes to test its weight and balance. He jammed the point of the blade into the ground and left the sword standing while he removed his own belt with its slim knife and handed it to Lio. The Kharnite took the belt, stood with it awkwardly. Balzan grinned and clapped his hand on Lio's shoulder.

"You think I'm going to lose, don't you?"

Lio started to protest, but his expression gave him away. Balzan chuckled lightly, tightening his grip on the Kharnite's narrow shoulder. "There are a few tricks I know that Kalak's never heard of, let alone seen," Balzan said quietly. "Just you watch, Lio. I'm not the dead man you think I am. Remember the Stalker, hmmm?"

He left Lio and crossed to the center of the rink, where Kalak was waiting impatiently, his arms folded across his massive chest, his eyes glaring. On either side of the Train-

131

er stood two soldiers, their features grim, fingering their own swords nervously, uncertainly. Balzan gave each of them a bright smile, then turned the smile on Kalak, who scowled.

"I'm ready," the young human said. "What about your friends?"

Kalak raised an eyebrow. "My friends?"

"The guards," Balzan said, gesturing at the soldiers with his sword. "Are they going to be here while we fight?"

"Don't you trust them?" Kalak asked dryly.

"Would you?"

For the first time the Trainer lost his scowl; his reptilian face broke open into a semblance of a grin, he turned and issued a curt order to the ranking soldier, then swung around to face Balzan once more. The guards moved from the rink and took up positions outside the ankle-high stone barrier which encircled the area. One of the guards gave Balzan a sour look. Mockingly, Balzan returned it.

The mockery almost cost him his life.

Out of the corner of his eye, he caught a glint of silver, something moving toward him, and he ducked, catching himself with a hand to the sandy floor of the rink. Kalak grunted as his neutron-sword went slashing through the air over Balzan's head, and for a brief second lost his balance, stumbling forward. Balzan came up, ramming his shoulder against the Trainer's breast bone; the two of them slammed backward, tripping and crashing to the ground, dust swirling up around them.

Kalak recovered first. Bracing himself, he shoved his left arm hard against Balzan's throat, just above the Adam's apple. The force of the blow stunned the young human, and he stumbled back, momentarily blacking out. Carrying through with the upward motion of his arm, the Trainer tossed himself upward and forward, sprawling over Balzan and grappling for the stunned human's throat. The sudden weight on his chest brought Balzan awake, and after a second of disorientation, he caught himself, managed to pull his knee up and jerked it sharply into Kalak's crotch. The Trainer wailed and fell away. Balzan scrambled to his feet, shaking his head against a haze of pain. By the time he'd focused, Balzan saw that Kalak was also upright, swaying, one hand clutching himself between his legs. The two men glared at each other, Kalak snarled through his agony and, like gaapur stags battling over a doe, they closed, swords swinging and sparking in the mist, ringing with the cacophony of metal on metal, steel on steel.

The battle seemed to rage for hours, but in fact, it lasted only several minutes. For Lio, watching from his place beside the water-trough, it felt like an eternity. Time and again, he was certain Balzan had fallen. Three times, the young human went down on one knee, and three times Lio started to step forward, ready to plunge against the Trainer, prepared—in effect—to commit suicide. And each time, miraculously, Balzan somehow forced the slashing neutron blade aside and regained his footing, and pressed the attack, taking the initiative once more. Still, the fight was taking its toll. Gradually Balzan's parries were slowing, his defense weakening. As Lio watched, he saw a line of sweat break past the leather band around his friend's forehead and trickle into the young human's eyes. Balzan's hand came up, his knuckles brushed the sweat away. And another line trickled down . . . and another . . .

Suddenly Kalak snorted triumphantly. His blade flicked out, its tip slipped into an opening in Balzan's guard and cut a red line down the youth's bare left arm. Blood welled in the cut, flowing freely along the forearm, spilling to the dusty ground. A pool quickly formed, arrowing toward the rink wall as Balzan took a step back, grimacing. The Trainer's brown eyes glowed, his jaws opened and his tight lips pulled back for a death's-head grin.

"First blood," he said. His voice was husky, a rumble that seemed somehow muted by the mist rolling in across the compound. "The man who draws first blood has his victory assured. Or haven't you heard that bit of wisdom, slave?"

"I was taught to wait until the last blood was drawn," Balzan replied between clenched teeth. "The man who makes predictions is a wishful fool."

133

"Then I'm a fool, slave," Kalak said, hissing. "For I tell you now: you're going to die."

"We're all going to die," Balzan said softly, "someday. Some die sooner than others. Some talk; others fight."

"Are you insulting me, slave?"

Balzan shrugged. "I thought you'd never notice."

He sidestepped the Trainer's enraged lunge, brought the flat of his sword down in an arc that ended in a slap on Kalak's rump. The Trainer howled in anger, whirled, swung his blade sharply toward Balzan's middle. Balzan jumped back, snapped his sword up to catch the reverse swing of Kalak's blade; the two swords struck, sparked blue in the mist, broke apart, came together again, and flashed briefly.

Kalak cursed, sucked in a breath, and visibly fought himself into an icy calm. Balzan smiled to himself; he hadn't expected the Trainer's unthinking rage to last, but while it had, it'd given him a moment's respite from Kalak's cold, considered attack. And that moment had been enough. He now knew what he must do if he was to return to his barracks alive. Gritting himself, he bore down and forced the attack closer to the practice area's short stone wall. If Kalak noticed the design behind Balzan's renewed assault, he gave no sign. They dueled in bitter silence, neither man taking his eyes from the other man's sword. For Balzan, it was as though the outside world had faded into the mist. All he could see was Kalak's blade, flashing in a blur before him.

He touched the wall with the outside of his foot; the stone was cool against his skin where it showed between the straps of his sandals. He had his back to the rink, to the water trough and Lio, and was just about to step over the stone rim when Kalak abruptly shifted his position, tossed his sword from his right hand to his left, and hooked his blade up against the hilt of Balzan's own sword—all in one smooth motion.

The edge of the blade sliced through the leather hilt, lopping the sword off a quarter of an inch above Balzan's fingers. The cutting edge of the sword thudded to the ground at Balzan's feet. He was left with the remains of the hilt—and Kalak, facing him, his reptilian features bursting with laughter at Balzan's horror.

4.

Less than a fifth of a second passed before Balzan reacted.

Like a cat, he pounced forward from the balls of his feet, diving against the Trainer, his stiffened fingers stabbing into Kalak's chest like sharp claws. Even as Kalak went down, Balzan leaped over him and raced across the packed earth of the practice rink toward the wash-trough. He paid no attention to the cry behind him, ignored the rasp of breath, the sounds of scrabbling as Kalak clambered to his feet, tail swishing out behind him. Balzan lowered his head and ran, his eyes riveted on the trough and on the weapons lying beside it. He didn't hear Lio call to him, though he sensed the young Kharnite's form rushing to his side. Without a word, he pushed Lio back and reached for the nearest weapon. It was a net, woven from strands of wire, light as a cobweb. He swept it up and turned. Kalak was almost upon him.

There wasn't time for Balzan to do more than avoid the Trainer's blows, and he was too close to the Kharnite to use the wire net properly; instead, he moved past Kalak lithely and once more broke into a run, heading across the rink toward the low wall. His feet slapped against the packed earth of the practice area, raising small clouds of dust, his footsteps loud in his ears, as loud as his breathing. Lowering his gaze to the ground, he watched for the short wall, crossed it, looked up as two guards hurried toward him, grabbing for their swords. He swung past the first one, smashed full into the second, knocking the soldier to the ground. Figures moved in the mist to either side of him, dim shapes that hardened into solid forms—the remaining soldiers of the guard Kalak had brought with him. Balzan gathered himself, swung the net low to the ground. The wire mesh tangled the legs of the three guards

135

to his right. All three men collapsed in a heap, the chin of the topmost guard clapping brittlely on the skull of the Kharnite under him. Without breaking stride, Balzan kicked in the bridge of the third guard's nose, shattering it. He jerked his net free, glanced over his shoulder, and ran on.

Ahead of him, the railing which marked the end of the stockade and overlooked the sprawled city below, glistened in the moonlight, beads of moisture from the mist catching the ashen light and glinting like bits of glass on the metal rungs.

Reaching the railing, Balzan came around, shaking the net out with one hand. He balanced himself carefully and waited.

Not ten feet away, Kalak stood motionless, watching him with narrowed eyes.

"To be honest, I never thought you to be a coward," the Trainer said, speaking slowly, his voice heavy and grating, "but it seems I was wrong. You've cornered yourself, slave. There's nowhere left for you to run."

"I've no intention of running," Balzan said.

"You're going to beg?"

Balzan shook his head. Kalak grunted. "It would have been useless, anyway," the Trainer said. "Under other circumstances, I might have let you live, with certain— modifications." He stared at Balzan's crotch pointedly. "But—" he shrugged "—we are none of us masters of our lives. Least of all, you, slave."

"Philosophy?" Balzan said sarcastically.

Oddly, Kalak didn't darken, he retained his calm and said, "No philosophy. Merely practicality."

With an almost resigned air—as though now that the question of the battle had seemingly been resolved, he'd lost interest in it—Kalak charged forward, his sword thrusting at Balzan's middle. There was no hatred on the Trainer's face; there was no expression at all.

Balzan moved. With one hand he brought up the net, catching Kalak's sword in its folds. With the other hand he clutched the Trainer's scabbard belt and pulled with a powerful twisting motion.

Now there was expression in Kalak's eyes: surprise.

136

Balzan caught a glimpse of another expression replacing the surprise, a look of comprehension and terror—and then the Trainer was past him, already tripping over the waist-high railing, plummeting forward into the air.

Propelled by Balzan's palm against his back, Kalak went over the railing. He was visible for at least half a minute as he fell toward the ground, lost in the mist and fog below. Then he was gone, without a sound to mark his passing . . . except a high-pitched scream that faded almost as quickly as it rose.

Chapter Fifteen

Trull put his hands on his hips, craned his neck backward to peer at Balzan with a sneer, and said, "He was a brutal fool, and he deserved to be killed, but you realize, of course, what this means for you: the pits."

Nervously Lio pressed against the guards arranged in a circle around the small group; within the circle, Trull stood glaring down at Balzan, who was held on his knees by two strong soldiers on either side; outside the circle crowded the yarrotites, awakened by Kalak's death-cry—the same death-cry which had summoned Trull. The newly promoted Kharnite soldier glanced at Lio and gestured for him to come forward. The guards stepped back and Lio entered the circle, looking anxiously from one unfamiliar soldier's face to another, finally resting his gaze on Balzan. The young human was tied securely—perhaps too securely. Red welts showed where the ropes bit into the skin of his arms; his head was pulled down until his chin touched his chest, held in place by a rope fastened about his neck and connected by a length of hemplike material to another rope at his waist. He was on his knees and swayed slightly as Lio watched. There were bloody bruises on his cheeks, forehead and neck; the skin across his back was cut from an impromptu lashing Trull had administered on his arrival; and he was bleeding freely from the cut along his left arm, the blood clotting to the remains of his clothes, dripping into a sticky reddish brown puddle at his knees. Lio shuddered. Balzan didn't return his friend's look, made no sign that he was aware of Lio's presence, until Lio spoke. Then the young human's head twisted to one side and he stared up from swollen eyes, his battered face expressionless—yet somehow, grim and determined.

"Master, it was a fair fight; the Trainer challenged him, a formal challenge he couldn't refuse."

"That may well be," Trull said, "but it's hardly to the point. Trainer Kalak has been killed; his murderer must be punished."

"What would you have had him do?" Lio asked, his voice breaking. "Let himself be killed?"

"That would've saved us all some trouble, wouldn't it?"

Trull's voice was cold. He took his hands from his hips and folded them across his chest, and returned his attention to Balzan, obviously amused.

"I'm not sure which I enjoy more," Trull said, "seeing you as you are now, completely humiliated . . . or thinking about how you'll be within a week, broken and mad, a cowering wreck of a man. You don't have any idea how much I despise you, outlander. You can't imagine how exquisite my hatred of you truly is."

"No greater than my hatred for you," Balzan whispered.

Casually, Trull swung his foot in an idle kick that caught Balzan's jaw and sent him reeling backward. When the guards had manhandled him back to a kneeling position, Balzan spat at Trull's feet, unable to reach higher. The Kharnite soldier laughed, and began to pace.

"I was willing to like you, outlander," Trull said. "I've always been an inordinately friendly man, eager to befriend a stranger, happy to give an outlander aid. That was a weakness; I know that now. And weakness is the one sin we must never forgive ourselves, no, never. You see, if a man is weak, then society is weak—" His eyes were brighter than normal, and his words had taken on a parroting rhythm; apparently, he was repeating something he'd been told, a painfully taught lesson. "—and a weak society can be the death of us all. You do understand that, don't you?"

He paused for confirmation. Balzan said nothing, only stared. Trull went on after a moment, more quickly now, pacing his speech to some mental drummer's increasing beat.

"When I learned you were a spy, a traitor, that you'd spoken against the traditions of Kharn and against Lord Sha, I was horrified. 'Can this be the man who asked my help? Is this the same man who questioned me like an innocent, who duped me with his play?' I realized, you see, that you'd lied to me. I saw you as you were and are —slime. A betrayer. No better than some thief who steals one's purse in the night, for what you stole was my misplaced kindness. You used me, outlander. I see that now. You used me, and I hate you for it—more than you can comprehend or hope to comprehend."

He turned and faced Balzan. His face had gone to a paler green; the lines across his brow and around his mouth were stretched taut over the contours of his skull; his eyes seemed to bug out from their sockets, muddy brown, tinged with yellow. Trull seemed gaunt. He looked ill, exhausted. His words seemed to come from a great distance, and echo within him before he spoke. Balzan gaped at him in dawning understanding, then pity. Trull was completely mad.

"No, you don't comprehend. Such subtleties are beyond you, outlander. You're coarse; a barbarian. That's what you are, a barbarian—and you used me—

"You used me!"

It was a scream, choking off into a stifled groan as Trull lunged forward, his claws slashing red lines across Balzan's throat as the Kharnite sought to strangle him. Jerking himself out of the loose restraint of his guards, Balzan butted Trull in the stomach, pushing him over onto his back. Trull hit the ground hard, the air exploding from his lungs, and lay there for several seconds with his eyes closed, breathing deeply through his nostril slits, raspingly. When he looked up again, his eyes had filmed over. His expression was totally devoid of emotion as he got to his feet, brushed the dirt from his tights and straightened his jerkin. He cast a disapproving glance at Lio, who remained in the circle, switching his glance from one to the other, from Trull to Balzan, and back again.

140

"Your friend is becoming violent," the Kharnite soldier said slowly, softly. "I'm afraid we have no choice but to take him down."

He walked from the circle, the yarrotites stumbling back to let him past.

A moment later Balzan followed, dragged by the ropes around his arms and chest, his feet digging a rut through the dirt of the stockade until he was borne to the gate, where the ground changed to the marble of the palace proper.

Lio watched them go, then hurried away to find Urro.

2.

They went down endless passages, through several arches each three times the height of a man, across a wide and dusty chamber lit only by the gloomy light from high-placed, grimy windows, and always down, down, until Balzan lost track of the number of rooms they entered and left, and all he could remember were ramps and spiral staircases. It seemed he'd been traveling forever through darkness. At first he made an effort to remember the path Trull took through the palace, then he abandoned the attempt, as it became obvious that the Kharnite was leading Balzan through a maze to confuse him. At length he shut his eyes, dizzied by the movement around him, though not too dizzied; he listened to the footsteps, to the echoes, to the whisper of a hundred curtains being brushed aside, to water dripping and distant ghostly cries. It was all he could do to retain what little energy he had left. Though beaten, he hadn't been broken; he was determined that somehow, he'd escape to free his fellows. He didn't know how; he only knew that it must be done, and so it would be done. Or he'd die in trying . . . which, as always, was a distinct possibility.

After a time, he realized that the air around him was becoming colder. There was a musty smell to it, like the odor one sometimes senses in an ancient cave far underground. Opening his eyes, Balzan surveyed his surroundings. The walls were made of stone, rough and hard here, with cracked edges and thick gobs of mortar holding them in place; elsewhere in the palace the corridors were composed of fine marble, expertly crafted and sculpted. Torches stood in niches in the walls, sputtering smokily, now and then flickering into momentary brilliance, then fading once more to a dull orange glow. The ceiling was lower than usual in the palace, and he noticed also that it was dripping. He shivered from the cold; it was at least twenty degrees below what was normal in the tower. His breath came out white with frost. He grinned at a sudden image, absurd in its clarity: he would freeze to death here, and his brittle body would be preserved forever. One day children wandering through the palace's lower levels would chance upon him, and wonder . . . who *was* this strange creature, whose skin was pink and hairless, whose bones were oddly shaped and who didn't even have the vestige of a tail?

Who, indeed? Balzan wondered. Once, he'd asked the Teacher that same question. "What is a man?" he'd asked, referring to his race. To himself. The Teacher had had no answer. In a way, that was one of the reasons why Balzan had come to Kharn seeking his friends; perhaps he'd also sought an answer to that question—a question, he realized, which had haunted him since the day he first stumbled on the Teacher, and understood how different from his tribesmen he really was.

"In here."

A door swung open. Balzan caught a glimpse of a small room briefly illuminated by the light from a torch on the wall behind him. It was barely high enough for him to stand in, barely wide enough for him to stretch out on the bare stone floor. There was a bucket in one corner; otherwise the room was empty.

A hand used a knife on the ropes binding him. Pain burned through his arms with the returning circulation. He started to rub his hand over his shoulder, grimacing from the pain—

Then something struck him hard behind his right ear,

142

and he spun forward into darkness. The cell door slammed shut behind him as he tripped into the tiny room. There was a clatter of metal against wood, slamming home into stone, and then silence. Balzan listened. Nothing.

He was alone.

3.

Heaving himself into the plush chair—designed for two adult Kharnites, but just right for *his* soft bulk—Trito let out a sigh and blinked lazily at the soldier before him. The soldier avoided the Gamemaster's scrutiny, keeping his eyes focused on a point above and to the left of Trito's head. It was the proper posture for respect, but for some reason it annoyed Trito; there was something about this Trull which disturbed the Gamemaster, some instability that worried him. Trull had been useful, extremely useful; but even a useful man can outlive his usefulness. Trito smiled at the thought and waved a hand for Trull to begin his report. The Gamemaster listened attentively, nodded when the soldier was done and said, "You've performed your duties well, Trull. Need I say that you will receive a reward in proportion to your service?"

The soldier bowed stiffly.

Oh yes, he's finished, quite finished, Trito thought. He gestured toward the door of the parlor which adjoined his bedroom, a wave of dismissal. He watched Trull leave, his pudgy lips pursed with a moue of disapproval. Something would have to be done about that man. At once; that very evening. It wouldn't do to have Trull crack and expose Trito's machinations to the queen; not at all.

Frowning with annoyance, at himself for thinking the task necessary, at Trull for making it necessary, Trito stretched and pressed a tab on the side of the table in front of him. Elsewhere in his apartments, a chime sounded. Trito heard it distantly, and relaxed in his chair, waiting for his servant to reply.

His face was the image of self-satisfaction.

"Mind if I join you?"

The soldier started. His hand tightened around his mug, and the sudden tension spilled some of the liquid within. The tall man standing beside the tavern table looked on sympathetically, waiting patiently for Trull to answer. After a brief inspection of the other man, Trull grunted and nodded at the bench opposite his own. "Sit if you want. It's no matter to me."

The tall man sat himself, caught the tavern master's eye and signaled for a mug of wine. While waiting for the tavern master to make his way through the press of drinkers mobbing the inn's sunken bar-pit, the tall man took off his hat—a cap, really, with the sigil of a Tradesman on its crest—and ran a hand through lank, thinning hair. Trull didn't seem to notice. The soldier kept his head lowered over his mug, withdrawn from the bustling around him.

"I was watching you, you know," the tall man said abruptly. Trull shrugged, without looking up.

"Why watch me, more than any other man?"

"Because you seem tormented. There aren't many men whose eyes are as bleak as yours."

Trull sipped at his wine. "My looks are my own business, Tradesman. And what's a tormented man to you?"

"A man is a man," the Tradesman said, "and a man in pain may need a friend."

"I have no faith in friends," Trull said. "Or in strangers who offer friendship."

"Bitterness?"

"I have my reasons."

The tall man's wine arrived. He accepted it, paid the tavern master and turned back to Trull. "Surely, you have your reasons. But are they good reasons? You can't judge yourself, you know. Tell me, and I'll judge for you. A man's always harshest on his own cause."

Something flickered in Trull's eyes, an emotion that flashed to the surface, then he was buried again. Dully, he said, "It won't seem like much . . . a minor thing, really . . . but it almost cost me my life, when Lord Sha learned about it. I could have died, thanks to this man. . . ." And slowly, haltingly, he told the Tradesman about the young human he'd met at the city gate; and the tall man listened, brow furrowed, his head inclined, nodding now and then. It was as though some burden were being lifted from Trull's shoulders as he spoke. His back straightened; his voice firmed; he seemed to regain lost energy. The tall man smiled kindly when he saw this. After a while, they began to talk of other things, Trull's bitterness forgotten. And when, two hours after their meeting, the Tradesman suggested they retire to another tavern not far away, re-knowned for its fine wine and finer women, Trull eagerly agreed. They went off, arm in arm, laughing at each other's stories.

It was the last time the soldier Trull was ever seen alive.

Chapter Sixteen

She'd been awake for hours, how many hours she didn't know, and the agony had long since become too much for her to bear. She'd stopped screaming shortly after Scala and Fayra caught her, when she'd realized that her shrieks of fear and pain were only exciting the females to greater efforts, and in all the time since then she hadn't uttered a sound, no word, no moan; she'd even managed to keep her breathing slow and even, and in a way this had been an agony almost as great as the physical pain Fayra inflicted. In all her years, Kitta had never experienced anything to prepare her for Fayra's sadism. The female's deft cruelty went beyond Kitta's most tormented nightmares. As some people took joy in craftsmanship, in jobs expertly done, Fayra took obvious delight in devising new methods of torture. She never made a permanent injury; such injury would have been evidence for Lord Sha; she would have been punished severely, perhaps executed, if Sha had ever found proof of the accusations made against her, and Fayra knew this, and worked accordingly. Her devices were delicate and left few—if any—scars.

Physically, that is.

Emotionally, there would be many scars. That was the point, after all.

At the moment, however, Fayra was joyless. She slammed her padded palm down on the top of the table on which she and Scala had strapped the Endorian female, cursing under her breath as she strode angrily about the small anteroom, attached to the female slave's quarters by one connecting door—now bolted. She swished her tail about, knocking over a low stool. From her place near the wall, where she'd stood with her hands clasped before her primly, Scala watched Fayra's performance with less than amusement. The reptilian female clacked her jaws together, glaring at Scala, then pointed at the table, Kitta upon it.

"Let me kill her and be done with it," Fayra said gratingly. "We'll get nothing from her tonight; she's as silent as a wall."

"I noticed. You've done everything?"

"More than everything. I've tried, but she's silent. When we first had her . . ." Fayra's expression lightened. Scala cut her short, pushing away from the wall and striding to the table. Kitta blinked up at her through a scarlet film. There was a cut in the eyelid of her right eye, the sort of cut one could receive by walking against a doorjamb. Blood welled from it now and then, obscuring her vision. Scala walked around the table, aware of Kitta's strangely sullen gaze.

"Perhaps you're right." Scala leaned forward, her fangs visible through slightly parted lips. "Have you learned fear yet, child? Are you afraid of us? Does the sight of Fayra's claws make you tremble? Well, child?"

Kitta said nothing. She was strapped to the table, held motionless, and she knew from experience she couldn't avoid one of Scala's vicious blows in such a position. The older female flicked her tongue over her lips, nodding slowly to herself. "You *do* fear us, I think, but you're clever, too clever." She glanced at Fayra, who stood near the door of the small room. "Are you hungry?" she asked the reptilian female; Fayra ducked her head in ascent. "Then we'll eat; perhaps later the child will be more receptive to our persuasion. We shall see."

Robes swirling, Scala strode from the room. Kitta watched her leave, and watched Fayra follow. When the door had closed behind them, she lay back on the table, stifling a moan, forcing herself to rest. She had a half hour—maybe more, but at the least, a half hour. It might not be enough time . . . but it was all the time she had.

The anteroom was low-ceilinged. There were no windows; three doors; a table, on which she lay; a stool, which was on its side in a corner; and a long couch, one which had once been in Lord Sha's quarters, but now—old and stained by countless pints of spilled wine—was used by the slaves; other than these few objects, the room was empty, a dusty unused chamber that resembled a tomb more than a place for the living. Kitta had already studied everything in the room, trying to distract herself from Fayra's tortures, and had found nothing which could aid her, but even so, she examined the chamber again, knowing she might have missed something. She gave up after several moments, sighing. It seemed she'd have to aid herself. Grimly, she set about squirming out of her bonds, ignoring the pain which shot through her with every motion of her right hand—which Fayra had worked over very carefully, spraining each finger and twisting the wrist, tearing cartillage but breaking no bones. Kitta gave no thought to what she was doing; ordinarily, she would never have attempted to escape, yet now she could consider no other alternative. Perhaps it was already too late, but she had to try to warn Balzan of Lord Sha's plans. It was no longer even a matter of choice.

By squirming and arching her body at impossible angles —Kitta, like all Endorians, was double-jointed—she managed to slip one hand free of the straps crossing her arms and chest. She snapped the lock on the leather strap across her breast, pulled her other hand free, and wincing against the pain, used both hands to remove the remaining straps. The table had been used in the surgery at one time, Kitta guessed; there were bloodstains, she noticed, on the sides of the long table—whether from operations performed by a palace surgeon, or tortures orchestrated by Fayra, she couldn't guess—and wheels at the base of the legs, locked in place. She climbed off the table, moving her limbs gingerly. Standing up, she almost fainted; her feet ached, and her eyelid wound began to pulse blood again as soon as she came upright; somehow she drew herself together and took a trembling step toward the door by which her torturers had left the room. Halfway to that door, she stopped. What if she met them returning? No, she'd leave by one of the other two doors. One of them had to be unlocked, and would lead to a main corridor eventually. From there she'd find her way to the stockade. Thinking this, she tottered across the room to the nearer of the remaining exits, fumbled the door open and stepped outside. She halted in the doorway, looking around her apprehensively.

She was in a passageway she'd never seen before. At one end was a high wooden door bearing Lord Sha's personal crest; at the other end, the passage turned to the right and vanished. The corridor was dark, lit by only one torch, several hundred yards away at the passage turning. Limping, Kitta started toward the torch, closing the anteroom's door behind her.

Dust coated the ground, rising as she walked over it, causing her to sneeze. Apparently this passage hadn't been used recently, at least in months. She left a trail of footprints behind her, a clear sign of the direction she'd taken, but her head throbbed so much and she was in such agony that she couldn't bring herself to take the effort to create a false path toward Sha's door. Let them follow her; suddenly she didn't care. Escaping had sapped most of her strength, leaving her only enough to force one foot in front of the other. She turned the angle in the passage and stumbled on through the pitch black. She came to a flight of stairs, went down them. As she stepped off the last stair, her balance fell apart and she collapsed in a heap against the cold stone wall.

She woke with a light shining brightly in her eyes. The light went away, and slowly the world came swimming into focus. There was a face somewhere above her, a friendly female face that expressed pleasure when Kitta blinked her eyes, and gave other signs of coming back to consciousness. It was a slave's face, a warm-featured slave in green silk robes. Kitta's returning sight brought her other details: she was on a lounge in a long, narrow room that opened at one end to a view of the city. There were benches along the walls, tables set before the benches.

Above her, hanging from gleaming bands of gold, were lanterns of ornate crystal. Marble was everywhere, and silk, and a sweet smell of perfume.

"Would you like to talk with her now, milady?"

"Yes. Leave us."

The slave's face rose up and passed from Kitta's view as the female left the room. Kitta swung her head about, saw another female approaching her. It was the queen, all in white and silver, pins and brooches clasping her wispy gown close to her body, her hair a sharp black against the snow-white of her garments. Her eyes were green, her skin milky. Kitta gazed at her, awed and frightened.

"You're one of Sha's concubines, aren't you?"

Kitta mumbled a yes, swinging her eyes away from the queen, her hands fidgeting with the cloth of her tunic.

"My girl found you outside the entrance to our slave quarters. You seemed hurt. She brought you here, with my permission of course. Frankly, I'm curious . . . has Sha taken to torturing his females?"

In a gush of words, uncertain why she was telling Myrane as much as she was, Kitta told the queen everything; about Scala and Fayra, and before she fully realized what she was saying, about Sha and Trito, as well. Myrane's features tightened during this last revelation. Her gaze became distant and cold, and she began to tap her hand impatiently on the arm of the chair in which she sat. Kitta finished her story breathless, and the queen folded her hands in her lap, staring at the girl and saying nothing.

"Can you stop them?" Kitta asked. "Before they hurt him, before they have him killed?"

Myrane waved a negligent hand. "Simplicity itself, child. As it happens, I've an interest in this Balzan."

Kitta started, then remembered what she'd overheard between Sha and Trito. "They said you'd be displeased if you learned their plans."

"And so I am, child," Myrane said. "So I am."

She seemed about to say something further, but pressed her lips into a fine red line, shook her head once and rose to her feet. "Stay here," she told Kitta. "Eat and regain

150

your strength. I may have a task for you shortly. We'll see what needs to be done."

With a sigh of gratitude and exhaustion, Kitta fell back on the low couch, closing her eyes and passing into a deep, secure sleep. At last, it appeared her troubles were over. But they were only beginning.

2.

In the nightmare he was alone on a deserted plain, an unnaturally smooth plain that stretched without relief from horizon to horizon, shining like metal under a starlit sky. A cool breeze ruffled the hair on his head, brushed his naked skin, brought a scent of something alien and yet familiar to his nostrils. He waited. Overhead, the stars stared down at him, a thousand gleaming eyes in the ebony night, watching him, accusing him. Gradually, a feeling of oppression built up inside him. Inexplicably, he found himself growing afraid, tense, uncertain. He tried to move, to run from the staring stars; he couldn't. His legs were rooted to the ground, and as he looked down at them in horror, the metal from the ground began to creep up his bare feet, extended pseudopods—gray and glistening—up his calves, reaching toward his thighs—

Screaming, he awoke.

A guard's head appeared in the slit in the door through which food was served. "Are you sick? You were shouting."

"Nothing," Balzan said. "Leave me alone."

The slit went dark again, the sound of the small panel sliding back into place reverberating in the cell.

He *was* alone, thought Balzan—completely alone on an alien world. He'd never thought of himself that way before, but in the days since the Alb attack on his village, he'd found himself growing more and more isolated—more and more alienated from the world around him.

Getting to his feet, he paced about the cell, able to take only a few steps before having to turn. He no longer felt

151

like sleeping; it wasn't that he was afraid of another nightmare, he was simply too tense, too restless for sleep. He stopped before the door, stood unmoving for several heartbeats, and then, suddenly, brought his fist up and smashed it against the jamb. He remained like that, breathing through his nose, almost panting, his fist planted on the cold stone; then slowly he relaxed, dropped his hand to his side, and returned to the corner where he'd been sleeping.

He sat crosslegged with his back against the wall, and faced the door, and waited.

Two minutes later, he got back to his feet, crossed to the door, and struck the jamb again, harder this time.

He went back to the corner, sat, waited two minutes, counting the seconds softly under his breath, got up, went over to the door, struck the jamb again.

After the sixth time, there was a clatter of keys outside the cell, a mumble of voices, curses, the sound of metal slipping into metal, the click of a lock—and the cell door swung open. A man stood in the doorway, silhouetted by the torchlight behind him. He cast about, caught sight of Balzan sitting in a corner, and started toward him.

The Kharnite had taken only two steps when Balzan came up without a word and smashed into him headfirst. The guard's breastbone cracked against Balzan's skull, and his spine shattered when the force of the young man's charge smashed him against the unyielding stone wall. He died instantly, a look of confusion replacing the grimace of pain scarring his face. Balzan let him slump into the cell, turned toward the corridor, and gaped as the door slammed back into place. Outside the cell there was an exchange of commands, a shout for help, the thumping of running feet. Balzan listened to the sounds and voices for a few minutes, but when it became clear that no one had any intention of opening the door to see about the fallen soldier, Balzan gave a disgusted grunt and glared at the Kharnite lying at his feet.

"You could have landed outside, you know," he said.

The dead man didn't reply.

By the following morning the Kharnite's body had begun to decay and the stench made Balzan too nauseous to eat the food thrust through the slit in his cell door. He pushed the plate of meal aside, took a long swallow of the fetid water which had been in his cell since his arrival and gave his companion a look that could only have been described as withering. Then he crawled back to his corner, crossed his legs and folded his arms, and thought. His eyes kept returning to the Kharnite, whose eyes were also open, though coated with a thin film and beginning to dry. For several moments they held each other's gaze, until Balzan finally broke away, got to his feet with a sigh, and crossed the small chamber to the dead man's side.

Bending, he started to turn the Kharnite over. He stopped suddenly, freezing into immobility. Something white with black markings crawled over the dead man's shoulder from the bloody pulp which had once been the Kharnite's back, and scrutinized Balzan unblinkingly with five small gray eyes. Its feelers twitched as it stood there on the corpse, six inches long, two inches wide, segmented, completely white like a slug, but for the black spots on its top. It halted about four inches from Balzan's left hand. He looked at it, his mouth twisting. As he watched, it scrabbled about, ducked its head back toward the green gore of the Kharnite's back, and resumed feeding.

With a cry, Balzan jerked the corpse to one side. The parasite fell to the ground and scrambled about excitedly, its feelers vibrating as it scurried about in short circles. Balzan brought his sandaled foot down on its back, clamping it down twice more. On the third blow there was a snapping sound, and something soft and white spurted from under his sole. He turned away, went into the corner furthest from where he slept, and was sick.

When he turned back, a second parasite was feeding on the broken remains of the first.

He didn't sleep, of course, but somehow he "woke" from a dream at a sound from the cell door. It had been another nightmare, the sort of nightmare one can get while still

153

awake; he'd felt himself falling into a pit where a thousand pulpy slugs waited to receive him, falling and screaming, though he fought to keep the scream down. The sound snapped him back to full awareness, yet for an instant he was disoriented. He sat straight, saw the sticky white clots which marked where he'd killed six of the slug-parasites, and for a split second he was back in his waking nightmare. Then the sound came again, and he jerked himself back to reality.

Someone was at the cell door, opening it.

Balzan came to his feet in one lithe movement, and slipped across the cell to a spot where he wouldn't be seen when the door was opened. He was less than a foot from the dead Kharnite's desiccated corpse, but this didn't bother him; he wasn't really aware of it. He held his breath and watched as the door eased open. A shadow stretched down the rectangle of light cast through the doorway onto the cell floor, a long, thin shadow of a figure in a hood and cloak. He waited until the source of the shadow had stepped fully into the cell, and then he jumped.

They fell to the floor in a tangle of arms and legs, of cloak and tunic. He managed to get on top of the intruder, was about to bring his fist around in a blow that would have crushed the other man's skull, when he stopped, startled to see that it wasn't a man at all.

It was a woman. He stared, unable to believe what he saw.

"Kitta!"

Chapter Seventeen

He helped her to her feet, his hand under her arm. She was pale under the light tan fur of her face, her eyes wide, one eye swollen and partially covered with a white bandage. She pulled herself against him and held his chest with her small hands, and cried, sobbing softly. He started to put his hand on her head, left the hand hanging in the air uncertainly. Finally he touched her, lowering the hood so he could smooth her fur, letting her cry against him.

While he held her, he craned his neck and glanced out the doorway. The corridor was empty as far as he could see in both directions. He returned his attention to Kitta, blinking down at her wonderingly.

"You came here by yourself?"

Her head moved, a brief up-and-down motion on his chest.

"The guard didn't stop you?" He broke in again before she could answer, "No, I suppose they didn't. You're here; that's proof of it."

He drew her away from his chest and tilted her face up in his hands. Streaks in her cheek fur marked the path of her tears. He ran a thumb under each eye, dabbing the moisture away. His hand paused under her injured eye. "Who did this to you? Was it Sha? Did he hurt you?"

"Not him," Kitta said gently. She explained about Scala and Fayra. Balzan frowned, scowling when she was done. She put her hand on his mouth before he could speak. "That isn't important now. I came to help you get away.

155

We have to leave before the Games begin; I was told the guards would come to take you to the huulat."

"The huulat doesn't worry me, Kitta. I've fought one before, and I'm still alive."

"Was it a Stalker?"

"That's what I was told."

"Then you didn't fight a huulat, not a true huulat. The slaves talked about them a great deal. The Stalkers are different, less ferocious beasts. They have to be, in order to be trained to work with Kharnite masters as trackers. You see that, don't you, Balzan? No one stands a chance against the arena huulat. Not even you."

Balzan changed the subject. "You seem to know a lot about these things, my sister."

"I've learned much since I came to Kharn," Kitta admitted quietly.

"Apparently," Balzan said. He caressed her face affectionately. "You've also learned a bit since I met you in the palace hall, and you told me you couldn't consider escaping from Sha. Here you are, talking about escape . . ." He laughed. "Why the change?"

"I couldn't allow them to kill you," Kitta said. She spoke simply, her shoulders lifting and dropping in a shrug, a matter-of-fact tone to her voice.

Balzan shook himself out of his reverie, and realized that he'd been staring at Kitta, and she at him, for several valuable seconds.

"Did you pass a guard when you entered?" he asked.

"No, I used a passage from the other direction, up from a lower level. It hasn't been used by the guards in years."

"Then how—" Balzan stopped himself from asking the obvious question; it didn't matter *how* Kitta learned about the "secret" corridor, only that she knew. "Can you find your way back there?"

"I think so."

"Then let's do so." He paused in the doorway, kicked at the corpse, now fallen on its side. "Sorry I have to leave you with *them*, friend. You've been an excellent companion, a worthy listener, and I wish there was something

156

I could do, but . . ." he smiled wryly, ". . . I have a more pressing engagement elsewhere."

The door slammed shut behind him and locked.

2.

The passage Kitta led him along was older than the one off which his cell opened. He almost had to crouch to pass under the lower beams which crossed the ceiling of the corridor, and once he bumped his forehead against an unexpectedly low arch. Kitta had little trouble negotiating the corridor, however, and moved ahead of him nimbly, pausing now and again to wait for him to catch up. "There're stairs not far from here," she told him at one point, as they stopped beneath a bared niche, in which a stumpy candle sputtered. Balzan looked at the candle briefly, wondering if Kitta had lit it on her way up the narrow corridor. "I'm going to take a slightly different route going back," she said, "to avoid anyone who may have followed me."

"Do you think anyone did?"

"It's a possibility," Kitta said, and moved on.

The stairs were as narrow as the corridor; narrower. Balzan brushed his elbows against the walls on either side as he followed Kitta's bobbing figure down the mossy steps, in a lazy spiral that led downward, toward a distant glow. He felt as though he were descending into the bowels of the palace tower, down into the intestinal depths. It wasn't a pleasant thought. He pushed it aside and concentrated on keeping his balance, which was becoming increasingly difficult as the angle of the steps grew steeper. He felt his way along, a hand on the clammy stone at his side, another probing ahead, and was glad when he swung his foot off the last step and moved out of the stairwell into a large, open chamber. It'd been too close in the well for his comfort. He took a deep breath of the musky air, gazing around him as he did.

He and Kitta stood at the far end of a huge reservoir, an immense circular pool covered with a layer of scum, that stretched into the shadows ahead and to either side. A ledge ran around the circumference of the pool, two feet wide at its narrowest point, a full ten or twelve feet broad here, at the base of the stairwell. The walls were all of stone, all neatly chiseled and set into place. Balzan shuddered as he looked about, however; there was something about the air in that place which gave him a chill.

"Where are we now?"

"Below the lowest palace level," Kitta told him. "This is the storage area for the tower; all of the drinking water is here. And beyond—" she waved vaguely "—are the purifiers, and the lifts to the topmost levels."

He shot a look at her, surprised. "You've been here before?"

"I told you; this is the way I came."

"Yes, but . . ." He let the sentence trail off uncompleted. There would be time for those questions after they'd reached the upper tower, after the Endorians had also been released. He had an idea how to deal with that situation: the arena, the Games, the huulats and the yarrotites—they would all be part of it, if he could only get there in time.

"The Games, Kitta—when do they start?"

"A few hours," she told him over her shoulder. "You needn't worry about them, really."

"Will the lifts take us to the arena level?"

Her eyes were odd and cold when she looked at him. "We won't be going by the lifts, Balzan. There's another way. I told you; we have to be careful, in case we've been followed."

"Which way, then?"

She pointed. "There. Along the ledge."

"I don't see anything. Just darkness."

"It's there," Kitta assured him. "A cross-tunnel which leads to an abandoned section of the tower."

"You're certain?"

"Yes." Kitta started off, not waiting to see if Balzan followed. He hesitated, brow furrowing. He moved to the edge of the platform, peered down at the clouded waters of the vast pool, shifted his gaze toward Kitta, already several yards away, then straightened and strode after her. He caught up with her as she turned to the left and disappeared through a circular tunnel.

Ducking, he followed her.

3.

... the tunnel, the muscles in the small from his stooped position, Balzan was ...... when he straightened by a sudden, intense light. He threw up a hand to protect his eyes, but it was too late. He was dazzled, and he stood helpless as the light receded; abruptly, the universe had become for him a flood of color, spots and dabs of darkness competing for dominance behind his eyes. He staggered forward, waving his hands, searching for something to hold onto, searching for Kitta. He called her name. There was no answer. A moment later the ground slipped away under him and he sprawled, cracking his jaw on hard stone.

He was up again almost immediately, sobered by the trickle of blood leaking from his split lip. He blinked his eyes, focused on several objects directly ahead of him. One was a humanoid form, a gracefully slim figure he recognized as Kitta. He lunged, grabbed the Endorian female's arm and swung her around. Between the splotches of light and dark still remaining from the dazzle which had blinded him, he saw her features firm into view.

She gazed at him calmly, without expression.

"You knew that was going to happen," he said tightly. "You didn't warn me, you lead me right into it. Why? What was that light, and why—"

"You might as well ask a statue, as ask her, outlander," said a soft voice to his side. Balzan whirled and found himself facing the queen. Myrane reclined in a throne not forty feet away; his vision still confused, Balzan was able to make out little else of his surroundings.

"You did this to her?"

"I did."

"I'll ask you, then: why?"

159

"I wanted her to bring you to me, Balzan. She's much too foolish a child to trust with such a task, without certain . . . conditioning. As herself, she would have panicked, possibly brought you elsewhere, or revealed my part in your rescue. None of that would have suited me. It was much simpler to temporarily shunt her own personality aside, and replace it with mine. When she arrived here, I regained my full ego, and the resulting energy dispersal . . . blinded you."

Balzan shook his head to clear it. Un Kitta, passed ▬▬ ▬▬▬▬ of response. "You hypnotized her," he said.

"Not quite. As I've already explained . . . I lent her part of my identity. It overwhelmed her, I'm afraid; for the moment at least, she's in shock." Myrane chuckled. "Which will not be inconvenient, I'm sure."

His vision clearing, Balzan started, shocked and somewhat awed by his surroundings. Since coming to Kharn, he'd seen a dozen, a hundred fantastic things, sights which had almost paralyzed him with wonder. The tall towers, the graceful architecture, the cesspools of the slums—each new experience had caught him by surprise, though always he'd managed to quell that surprise before it swamped him. Now, again, he stood and gaped at the chamber his returning sight revealed to him; and for one heart-stopping moment he was rooted to his place, unable to turn his thoughts away from what he saw.

It wasn't so much a room as a cavern, a man-made cave several hundred feet high, several hundred feet wide, extending far back into the distance, the ceiling dropping to meet the floor at some gray point ahead of him. Slender, sculpted columns thrust up toward the faraway ceiling, long white lines that rose dizzily into the overhead shadows. Each column sported twisting figures cut from marble, demons, male and female, contorted around each other in a spiral toward the ceiling. As he stepped forward, staring, Balzan saw that each of the sculpted figures was different, though all were humanoid. Some seemed based on a reptilian race, others were catlike, a few bore wings, horns, long ridges of bone riding down the skull along the neck, hooves on gaapurlike legs, and eyes that seemed to watch and follow him as he moved closer or turned away. There was something about those figures which disturbed some ancestral memory deep within him. It seemed to him that the demons portrayed in the polished marble were alive; merely frozen in place, not created from lifeless stone. It was a thought that persisted even after he'd torn his gaze away.

The floor beneath his sandals was also of marble, huge squares of white and tan stone set flat and flush together, blue veins winding a path through the glistening floor, like azure serpents caught in pale amber. Balzan shivered involuntarily and lifted his eyes to stare at the other outstanding feature of the bizarre chamber.

A hundred feet away there was a pool—or rather a pit. It was square, with a rim of black stone edging it, and a platform rising from a point in its center. Balzan walked to the edge of the pool, drawn less by curiosity than a growing suspicion, a dull horror he found he couldn't resist. He felt like a bird walking toward the open mouth of a snake, aware of the waiting fangs, aware that death loomed before it . . . but helpless to resist the lure of the snake's mesmerizing eyes.

Reaching the black rim, he paused, and looked down into the waters of the pool. His reflection mocked him with a blank expression.

The "water" was a deep, rich red.

The color of fresh blood.

Myrane's voice, silky and oddly without an echo, brought him sharply from his reverie.

"Perhaps now you begin to understand, Balzan of Endore. Come to my side, and I'll tell you more, answer your every question."

He lifted his head. "Every question, my queen?"

"All." Her green eyes sparkled; she held out a hand, motioned with it languidly. "Sit here beside me." Her other hand touched the stone throne to her left, a chair similar in every way to the one on which she sat, though resting on a platform lower than hers. Its arms were of some pink stone, its back and seat of black and white leather; here too, the demon motif was repeated, in a horned head which rose from the back of the throne and peered across the shadowed chamber. Balzan walked across the expanse of marble floor, halted before the twin thrones and slowly shook his head.

"I'll stand," he told Myrane. "If my queen doesn't mind?"

"Do as you will," the queen sniffed. "This is the second time you've spurned me. I promise you, it will also be the last."

"You said something about answering questions?"

"In my own time, in my own way." Balzan noticed that Myrane seemed to have lost interest in him for the moment, and he took the opportunity to study the rest of the vast room, visible behind her.

There were no other exits, he saw, though there was something of an altar against the far wall, steps leading up to a slab of silver set on four short stubs of pink stone. On either side of this "altar" there were vases, each large enough to contain a man—or so it seemed to Balzan— and each cut from some black, opaque material that absorbed the light, unreflected. Above the vases two globes stood out from the wall, each three times the size of a man's head, each glowing and providing the chamber with its illumination; the light the globes gave off was a gentle blue, the color of water in an inland pond. The thought of water reminded Balzan of the pool; he turned and examined it once more, just beginning to comprehend that the pool was the source of the uneasiness which seemed to overpower him.

The pool. And in the pool, a platform. He'd seen the platform before, but hadn't really been aware of it, his attention stolen completely by the red liquid surrounding it. The platform was formed of gold, and rose over the pool on three slim legs, its base just touching the surface of the scarlet "water." It was circular, a round stand, concave in the center. Resting in the concavity was an egg-shaped object the color of a pearl, a milky white that shaded to a light gray at its fuller end. But neither the stand nor the egg-object itself impressed Balzan. What held him were the jewels imbedded in the egg, seven crimson stones arranged neatly, equidistant from each other, in the egg's skin. Seven red gems gleaming dully in the soft blue light. Seven stones.

"You understand now, don't you?"

He didn't look up; he continued to stare at the jewels. To his side Myrane laughed distractedly.

"You heard about them; now you see them," said the queen's gentle whisper. "The blood stones.

"The seven jewels of blood."

Chapter Eighteen

As though from a distance, Balzan heard the queen speak, and with a sense of growing apprehension he listened, believing without question what she told him:

"I notice that the liquid in the pool also fascinates you; but surely you've seen it before, a man like you, so accustomed to the horrors of the battlefield, so familiar with your enemy's blood. It *is* blood, Balzan, the blood of your fellows, the yarrotites who have preceded you and your friends to the arena so far above. How many men died to fill that pool? A thousand. Two thousand? Numbers have little meaning after a point. They died as they lived, my outland friend, fighting to save their futile lives, and now their warriors' blood serves a higher purpose than filling their veins. It maintains the life of Myrane and keeps this foul city, this foul kingdom, in my control.

"In *my* control, Balzan of Endore, not in the Red Lord's, or in Sha's. This Kharn is in my hand as Sandar was in my mother's, and Ki in my grandmother's, and Simu in my great-grandmother's, and on backwards through the history of this world, a city commanded by each female of my line, back to the dawn of time.

"Sandar. Let me tell you of Sandar, outlander, so that you may understand the woman who sits upon the throne before you. One thousand years ago the city-state of Sandar was at its peak, a kingdom which sprawled over half a continent, an empire which controlled a hundred colonies, each an island in the mighty ocean to the north of Kharn. Sandar had grown from a small duchy much like Kharn, had developed a science and technology beyond anything your feeble mind can imagine, was beginning to reach out, to gather in more power and wealth, more food, more resources, with each passing week and month; within a decade, it would have been the most powerful kingdom this world has ever seen, a kingdom to rival all the kingdoms which have sprung up through eternity, to rival and surpass the greatest empires of all time. I told you it occupied half a continent, but did I tell you where? No? Then listen: once there was a land mass in the center of the vast Northern Sea, a plateau reaching from the darkest depths of the ocean, rising like some immense beast from the purple waves. This land mass was three times the size of Kharn's entire kingdom. There were rolling hills, valleys, plains of grass . . . it was perhaps the most beautiful part of this planet, a garden in the midst of a warm sea. The seasons were balanced and regular, the summers warm and mellow, the winters cool and short. Crops were plentiful, water everywhere, in a thousand springs and rivers, a dozen large inland lakes and ponds. Animals of every kind known in Kharn lived there, and some unknown in Kharn. The people of Sandar were gifted with strength and endurance, and blessed with health and long life. Without a doubt, it was one of the loveliest of this world's lands. So it was before my mother and her mother came to its shores; and under my mother's rule, Sandar prospered, and added man-made beauty to its natural beauty. Towers reached toward the pale sky, roads wound beneath earth-brown hills, fields were planted and agriculture flourished; it was a golden time, Balzan. A time of power and love. It lasted fifteen hundred years; then the trouble came.

"In every era there are men and women who are dissatisfied with life, who turn against the pleasures they know, in search of new pleasures and unknown dreams. They pretend they seek fulfillment of their petty hopes and aspirations, but in truth, they wish only to destroy the hopes and aspirations of others more worthy than themselves. Such was the case in Sandar. Men and women began to spring up who hated the way my mother ruled their kingdom. They didn't see the beauty she'd created;

only the squalor they'd made of their own lives. Because they were not so fortunate to have been born a member of the aristocracy, they demanded that the aristocracy fall, that it be crushed, that *they* gain power instead. They refused to listen to my mother's entreaties and they were immune to the influence of the blood jewels. . . . They revolted, and there was war—a long nightmare of war that eventually crushed the joy of Sandar . . . left the kingdom in ruins . . . sank that massive continent . . . and forced my mother and myself, at that time only a small child, to flee.

"After a hundred years of wandering, of passing from one unsuitable kingdom to another, of wondering if we would ever find a land where we could rule as we were born to rule, we came here. My mother died then, as all the older women of our family die, when they've brought their daughters to their new homes, and I took up the mantle of my ancestors, allowed the Red Lord to court my favor and marry me, and now, through him, and with the aid of the seven stones you see below . . . I rule a kingdom of my own. A kingdom which will one day equal the majesty of Sandar. And who can say, perhaps one day, gain majesty beyond that long-dead empire's most fevered dreams."

She paused. Balzan rubbed a hand along the side of his jaw thoughtfully, avoiding her gaze. Finally, he broke the silence and said, "What about the stones?"

"The stones? The blood stones?"

"You've mentioned them a dozen times; you imply they've always been with you. What are they, how do they fit into this story of yours?" As he spoke, he cast a look over his shoulder at Kitta, who remained immobile near the tunnel entrance, a slim, sickly figure in a dark robe and cowl. He swung around when Myrane answered his question.

"The blood stones are the key," said the queen. "Without them, this would all be but a fantasy."

Balzan started to comment, but held himself, wisely.

"How so, milady? What are they?"

She sighed and leaned forward in her throne. The movement caused her breasts to thrust against the fabric of her gown, outlining the small twin dots of her nipples, a somber red against the white of her bosom.

Her nostrils flared, her eyes flickered emerald, and she said, "They are older than you or I, and I am older than you can imagine. They were created before the dust congealed to form this planet; they existed when our sun was a bloated red giant; my mother believed they were and are as old as time itself. Within each of those stones there exists power enough to destroy this city and a hundred like it; also within each jewel, there lies the secret of eternal life . . . a secret known by my mother, and her mother before her . . . down to the first forgotten woman who came upon these stones in some dark field, on a night lost in the ages of prehistory. Perhaps they are the remains of a meteor which crashed on our world eons before life evolved; perhaps they are a gift from whatever gods pretend to rule this insane cosmos. I neither know nor care. I understand their properties; I know how to coax forth the rays which extend a life past its natural limits; and I know how to feed the jewels with living blood, to keep them fresh and pulsing with energy. In return, the jewels provide me with life, and the blood I give them, when distilled in a proper manner, becomes a powerful drug . . . which soothes the people of Kharn. Each feast—a feast given once a month before the Games —the citizens of Kharn are given a dose of this drug in their food. It serves to make them more passive, more accepting of their lot in life. Even the palace servants and retainers, even Lord Sha and that fat, repulsive Trito, even the ladies and gentlemen of the Red Lord's court: all receive their monthly dose, and thereafter all are quite amenable to the Red Lord's rule. And, in turn, the Red Lord is quite amenable to me."

There was a moment's silence while Myrane's voice drifted off, and she looked into the distance, her eyes focused on some sight invisible to Balzan.

"Blood," she said softly, her voice almost too low for the young human to hear. "The blood of the genetically

167

pure, Balzan; this is what the seven stones must have, this is what they must bathe in, if they are to give off their life-providing rays. Not the blood of just any animal, but the blood of a sentient being, a strong, intelligent being; the sort of man who would survive the Games despite all odds. A man such as you," she finished, her eyes resting on him. He shifted uncomfortably, aware that he was unarmed, and feeling naked for it.

"I wondered about that," he said. "No one seemed to know what happened to yarrotites who came out of the Games alive. They were supposed to be freed . . ."

". . . but they ended here, instead." Myrane's laughter was a light tinkling in the vast hall. "You're the first man who's ever resisted the gift of my favor, Balzan. Many former yarrotites have sat on this throne beside me and, for a night, possessed me. As I possessed them, that eve and forever after. It's a circle, you see. A cycle. The blood from the pool drugs the people, keeping them loyal and unthinking; in turn, the people provide the yarrotites from among their ranks, and the yarrotites provide the survivors, men powerful enough to live through the Games; and the survivors provide the blood, which provides the stones with energy; the stones emit radiation, which allows me to live, and mutates the blood into a drug; and the drug keeps the people . . . *mine*."

"If that's so," Balzan said, "what went wrong in Sandar, and all those other cities you mentioned?"

"For the others, I cannot say. For Sandar . . ." She shrugged her delicate shoulders. "An act of fate, of the gods, if you will. There was an earthquake which shook the palace, cracking the pool in which the blood stones were held; the life-giving blood drained off; before we could call the Games, the people—without the drug to calm them—revolted. There was death, fighting in the streets, chaos—"

"We?"

"What?" She drew herself back from the past, looked at him.

"You said *we*. I thought you were only a child at the time."

168

Coldly: "I was, outlander. Do you presume to question me?"

"Not at all." Balzan mused, rubbed his jaw again. "What was your mother's name, Myrane?"

The queen froze into immobility. "I don't believe I'll answer that."

"You won't, because you can't."

"Enough."

He pushed ahead. "You can't, because you don't know . . . because your mother died so long ago, you've *forgotten* her name."

"I said enough. Do *not* disobey me, outlander."

"How old are you, Myrane? How old are you, really? You implied that you were at least five hundred years old, old enough to remember Sandar—"

"Be quiet! I'll hear no more of this!"

"—but perhaps that's too modest; perhaps you're even older—"

"I warn you, Balzan of Endore. There are matters of which I've not told you, secrets too terrible for your mind to hold."

"—a thousand years old, two thousand? Or are you older, Myrane? So old, even *you* don't remember? Could you be the primitive female who first found that fallen meteor, in the days of the Old World? How old would that make you, my young queen?

"As old as Evil Itself?"

2.

The queen went rigid in her pink-stoned throne, and in that instant Balzan knew that he'd gone too far. Much too far.

There could be no turning back.

He let out a breath and balanced himself on his toes, waiting for the attack he knew would come, but unsure which direction it would be launched from. His hands clenched into fists, and he cursed the lack of foresight which had allowed him to leave the cell area without stealing a knife from a guard; he'd trusted Kitta, and now, because of that trust, he would probably die. No, not probably; he corrected himself. Only possibly. As long as he was alive, as long as he could fight, he had a chance. An Endorian might have surrendered himself to Myrane's mercy, but Balzan would rather die bloodied and in pain than to live a few more hours as the queen's slave.

Uneasily, he kept the queen's gaze, ready to move at the slightest motion around him. Seeing this, Myrane smiled thinly, the rest of her face remaining expressionless, and laughed.

"Outlander, you still delude yourself, don't you? You still believe this to be a game in which a man may win through skill or stroke of chance. Not so. The moment you entered this city, your fate was cast. Every action, every effort on your part, has been only to bring you to this moment . . . to your death." Noting his look, she said, "You think not? Very well. Let me ask you, Balzan: how do you suppose I overpowered those yarrotites who came to this chamber before you? They were all large men, some larger than yourself. Did you imagine I captured them myself?"

Balzan's eyes narrowed as he guessed what was coming next. "To be frank, I haven't given it any thought."

"You should have," Myrane said. "Perhaps you would have expected Juuk."

"Juuk?"

"That's right, outlander. Behind you." And she cried out something in a language that sent shivers up his spine, a tongue with words that stirred some forgotten racial memory—something Balzan couldn't explain, since he wasn't a native to this world; but then—neither were the blood stones.

Yet, even as he heard Myrane's brief warning to look behind him, he was already turning, pivoting on the ball of his foot soundlessly, like a cat. At first his eyes shot glances toward every corner of the room, toward the tunnel through which he and Kitta had entered, toward the surface of the blood pool, and toward the shadows stretching from the sculpted columns. A low, slow, sucking sound

170

brought him swinging back. He looked around aimlessly, seeing no one. The sucking sound continued, and he lowered his glance, and suddenly froze as he saw what he'd missed before—

A thick, crooked arm reaching from the pool toward the black stone rim. Blood drained from the hair matting the knobby hand; another hand came up to join the first; both hands gripped the ebony rim and heaved, drawing a massive black body from the scarlet liquid. As Balzan stared, a flat head appeared, then sloping shoulders, a barrel-chested torso, hairy genitals, and legs that were each as thick as Balzan's waist. The creature's feet ended in hooves. It swung a narrow tail from the base of its spine. Its black, pitted eyes carefully surveyed the chamber, finally settled on Balzan. Its mouth opened, baring wicked fangs. The creature had no nose, no ears, its head —like the rest of its body—was covered with blood-soaked hair, hanging in shaggy bangs across what little brow it possessed, draping its wide shoulders, reaching down its back and chest like black tentacles caressing the beast's filthy flesh. The creature stank with mold and decay; the odor rose from it like a physical threat. Balzan took a step backward to get away from the smell. Grinning with its hideous fangs, the creature followed him, matching Balzan step-for-step until the young human halted, glaring at the queen.

"Juuk is my slave, Balzan of Endore. A demon created from one of the unfortunate yarrotites brought into my presence. Instead of being dissolved by the blood pool . . . he *changed* into the creature you see before you. He's quite useful, in his own way. He lives only to fight. And to serve me. As I say, he is my slave."

"Oh?" said Balzan, readying himself. "I thought he might be your lover. You both have so much in common, you know . . ."

Myrane arched from her throne, spitting and hissing like a beast. She cried out in the language she'd used a moment before, and Juuk snuffled and growled, low in his heavy chest. Balzan tensed, watching the muscles ripple

171

along the creature's legs and sides. Juuk shuffled forward. Balzan moved to meet him.

A second later they were at each other's throats.

For many years Juuk had lived in darkness, a shadow-world unrelieved by light of any kind, where he cowered in fear of every sound and unfamiliar scent. He was not a brave creature at those times; only when the Soft One came, and spoke to him in a tongue he could understand, did Juuk gain courage, gain, in fact, a bestial fierceness that matched—in a way—the intensity of the cowardice he normally felt. When the Soft One whispered to him, it was as though Juuk were transformed: he became stronger, and grew to almost twice his size, and for a few moments at least, he could almost remember a time when things had been different, when he'd lived in light always, and not for just brief minutes that passed before he could fully savor their delight. Almost, it was as though there were *two* Juuks—and for some reason, this thought frightened him—one of whom existed inside his mind, deep down in some hidden corner, and the other—who lived in darkness, waiting to be awakened from his fear-filled sleep.

This thought confused him, for it implied things he couldn't comprehend. For instance, if there were two Juuks—a hidden Juuk and a frightened Juuk—which Juuk was the proper owner of his body? Could two Juuks exist, and both be real? Or was only *one* Juuk real, and the other merely a phantom . . . a ghost? He couldn't know the answer, and wasn't certain he wanted to know. It was all beyond him.

But if one Juuk was real, and the other only a phantom —*which Juuk was he?*

With a snarl of repressed rage, he went for the man-thing before him.

Killing was something he could understand.

Balzan broke away from the bloody creature and circled him, watching for some opening in the creature's defenses, something he could use to gain the upper hand. He was helpless against those slashing claws and biting fangs, and without a sword or his therb he didn't stand a chance. He'd be slaughtered. Torn to pieces. An image flashed into his mind, a mental view of his body after Juuk finished with it—and the picture he conjured wasn't a pretty one. Whatever Juuk had been before his transformation, the creature he'd become was certainly carnivorous. And the young human was a prime piece of meat. . . .

No, Balzan thought suddenly, *I won't let it end like this. The others can lie down and die . . . but I'm a man, dammit!*

"I'M A MAN!"

He realized he'd shouted that last thought aloud, and Juuk was gaping at him in astonishment. Before the creature could regain his defensive stance, Balzan attacked. He launched himself forward, grabbed Juuk's sodden arm and spun the creature around, his foot darting out and making contact with Juuk's shin just above his hoof. There was a sharp *crack!* as Balzan's stiffened toe connected with bone, snapping Juuk's shin, crumpling the creature to the ground. Instantly Balzan was on him, locking his arms in a full nelson up through Juuk's armpits, his hands clasped together over the back of the beast's neck. Juuk snarled and snapped, grunting with pain as the two of them tossed about on the marble floor. The creature kept trying to twist around to sink his sharp fangs into Balzan's forearm—but the full nelson was too firm, and Juuk's jaws clacked together on empty air, time and time again. Slowly, inexorably, Balzan began to apply pressure. . . .

When Juuk's neck broke, the sound seemed to explode amid the grunting and scuffling, and for a moment there was utter and complete silence in the cavernous chamber.

Then, softly, there was a sigh, as Juuk released his last breath. And across the room, a cry—as the shocked queen drew one in.

The beast's eyes rolled up.

He was dead.

And suddenly, in the midst of the darkness which enveloped him, there was a brilliant burst of light. For the first time since the blackness enfolded him, many, many years before, Juuk *understood*.

And in the moment of comprehension, as he realized what he'd been and what he'd become, as he remembered his days as a thinking being, as sweet memories of soft breezes and gentle hills came sweeping in on him—

The darkness returned and swallowed him forever.

Myrane stared at the young human, rising from the corpse of the slave who'd served her so well, for so long. Dully, she watched the blood-stained youth bend and lift the dead Juuk onto his muscled shoulders, watched as he strode with the creature toward the black edge of the scarlet pool. And as Balzan stepped onto the ebony rim, and shifted the weight he held propped over his head, Myrane guessed what he planned to do, and opened her mouth to scream.

With one tremendous shrug, Balzan hurled Juuk's corpse toward the pearly egg at the center of the blood pool. The body turned once, long arms flailing, and then struck the golden platform heavily, smashing into the egg with all the weight of its three hundred pounds. The egg cracked.

The world imploded.

Chapter Nineteen

Balzan was never quite certain what happened next. It seemed to him as though the entire universe had rushed inward toward one tiny point, a funneling of power and matter that swept him up and carried him along like a chip of wood caught in a hurricane. Directly before him he saw a glowing circle—almost a hole in space—a circle of white brilliance that drew in the power roaring at it from all sides, sucking it in like a drain sucking water. All around him, there was the sound of an enormous explosion—noise that went on and on, battering him as he whirled. An eternity passed in that single instant as the egg containing the blood stones split open, and the forces contained within it escaped—not outward into space, but inward, to some other dimension. How long the implosion lasted, he would never know; perhaps a second, perhaps a minute—perhaps an hour. While it lasted, he existed in a nightmare.

Then, as abruptly as it began . . . it was over. Done.

The winds which had borne him ceased to exist; he fell heavily to the marble floor, as around him the earth buckled and groaned, shaken to its very foundations. The unending sound of the explosion vanished, to be replaced by other sounds, more familiar, though no less frightening: the deep rumble of an earthquake beginning in the fissures below the palace tower, and the nearer, more ominous sounds of cracking columns, splitting walls, collapsing ceilings. He looked up from the floor, his eyes blurred with tears caused by the wind. When he wiped them away, he saw Kitta lying not far from him, her cowl thrown back exposing her delicate features, her robe split, revealing her furred legs and bare feet. He hurried to her side, saw that she was only unconscious, not seriously injured. As he straightened, the column nearest him sagged, fell outward, crashing to the marble floor and shattering into a thousand shards. He turned, gaping at the chaos which was turning the cavern into a ruin. His eye fell on the blood pool, now completely drained, its barren pit stark and empty, its golden platform a twisted ruin, the egg-pearl and the blood stones—

Gone.

"You have destroyed me!"

The cry came from the direction of the queen's throne. Balzan turned that way, and started when he saw Myrane, lying yards from the broken remains of the two massive chairs. She was on her stomach, her silky gown lost in the violence of the blood stones' implosion. Naked, she seemed smaller somehow. Her long black hair covered her back and lay in a halo around her shoulders, and draped her face in a curtain, which moved slightly as she breathed in short, shallow gasps. Balzan approached her warily. He stopped more than an arm's length from her hand, which scrambled toward his foot like a pale white insect. "Don't," he said softly. Myrane froze. He moved a step closer, bent.

There was a shudder in the chamber around them.

"All is gone," the queen whispered. "All is ruined. A million years, the dreams of a thousand centuries." Her voice was practically too low for him to hear, and almost drowned in the crumblings and crashings which echoed through the cavern. "You have destroyed me . . . do you realize what you've done . . . you have destroyed me. . . ."

The whispering continued, inaudible now.

Balzan returned to Kitta and tenderly lifted her in his arms. She was as light as a child. Her eyes opened, the lids moving sluggishly, as though she were drugged. "Balzan?" Without waiting for an answer, she pressed closer to him, clutching his chest with her small hands, still only half-conscious. Her eyes closed; she passed into sleep. A normal sleep, Balzan noted gratefully. Myrane's influence was gone.

At the thought of Myrane, Balzan glanced toward the queen's huddled form. A jagged bit of stone fell from the ceiling, smashing into pieces not a dozen feet from where she lay. He took a step toward her, starting to shift Kitta's weight so he could place her over his shoulder and free the other shoulder for Myrane—but came up short, his mouth opening and his eyes widening.

The queen was *shriveling*.

As he watched, her smooth skin began to wrinkle and shrink, drawing tight over sharp bones, cracking redly in hairline fissures over her arms and back, across her buttocks and along her thighs and calves. Not only was the skin drying, withering, but the very *shape* of Myrane's body was also changing. Her shoulders began to round, her back to twist and contort, her legs to tighten up into a fetal crouch. Blue veins popped out across her skin, exploding a network of purple lines over her limbs and around her now sagging breasts. Her hair dropped from her skull, and what remained went from a rich black to a sickly gray, to a crisp white—and then that hair too fell out, and the once beautiful queen was bald, save for a few scraps of white dotting her brown-spotted skull. She began to scream then, apparently becoming aware of the change for the first time, as a shock victim only becomes aware of the pain of an injury after he becomes aware of himself. Her screaming went on, finally broke and became a whimper, as one by one her teeth slipped from her gums, and her mouth became a red and bleeding mass. Balzan stared, horrified. She seemed to see him with her rheumy eyes; there was a pleading in those eyes, but there was nothing, nothing he could do. Except watch. And he watched, realizing what was happening.

The queen was aging. "A million years, a thousand centuries," she'd said. In the span of a few moments, she was catching the full brunt of Time. . . .

Now the skin peeled back like parchment from the old bones, and even the whimpering was ended; the parchment collapsed into dust, and the gray, dry bones rapidly followed. Soon only a fine ash was left of the emerald-eyed Myrane. Ash, and Balzan's memories.

177

Slinging Kitta over his shoulder, he turned on his heel and left, running as the chamber collapsed behind him.

2.

He found the lifts where Kitta had indicated they would be during their escape from the prison level. Chunks of stone and clouds of mortar fell around them as Balzan negotiated the narrow path between the water purifiers, one particularly large stone landing directly before him, forcing him to detour around it—a maneuver that Kitta's slack presence on his shoulder made no easier. The lifts were in a niche away from the main chamber, in which the purifiers and the underground reservoir were the dominant features. He strode up three steps to the platform on which the lifts loaded and unloaded, and ducked as a shower of dust cascaded from above. There was a roar somewhere in the distance, a ripping sound, and a section of ceiling came away and fell into the reservoir, splashing water everywhere. Coughing, Balzan groped into one of the lifts, pressed a tab set into the cylindrical wall and slammed to his knees as the lift shot upward. The abrupt acceleration made him drop Kitta, and she fell against the curving wall, bumping her head awkwardly and stunning herself awake. She blinked at him groggily. He smiled. Beneath them, the lift surged upward, sending their capsule rocketing toward the arena level hundreds of stories above.

"I was afraid for you," she said.

"I know."

"Lord Sha said he wanted to kill you. They were going to have one of the Trainers—"

He put his hand on her knee. "I know," he said again, more softly.

She looked at him curiously. "It was the queen, wasn't it? I felt there was something wrong when I went to her. I fell asleep . . ."

Briefly, without describing the more grotesque details, he told her what had happened in Myrane's chamber, beginning with Kitta's appearance in his cell. Throughout the explanation, the young Endorian listened blankly, and when he'd finished, Balzan noticed that there were tears in the female's eyes. "If she'd killed you, it would have been my fault," Kitta said. "Everything that's happened to you has been my fault; your coming here, being captured ...now this...."

"People do what they want to do, Kitta. No one forced me to come after you and the others."

"I wish I could believe you," she replied. "I can't forgive myself."

"Try," he said. "Try to understand how it is with me...."

Before he could finish the thought, there was a hiss, a deep hum, and the lift capsule began to slow. Balzan gestured for Kitta to get to her feet, and climbing to his own, faced the oval exit portal. The lift slid to a stop; the portal opened. A Kharnite soldier was standing outside, looking worried, an expression that switched to one of surprise as Balzan stepped from the capsule, casually reached out and struck the Kharnite across his massive jaw. Balzan caught the soldier's belt as the Kharnite fell, jerked the man's sword free and let the Kharnite drop the remaining distance to the floor. Then Balzan swung the sword in an experimental arc. "It'll do," he said to himself. Looking up, he saw two more soldiers rushing toward them across a vibrating rooftop. In the distance, Balzan could see the swooping outer wall of the arena; overhead, there was sky, no ceilings, no high tower. They were on the topmost level of the palace. They were also under attack.

Kitta watched in awe as Balzan disposed of the two Kharnites in a quick flurry of clashing swords; sparks flew, metal rang; and when all was done, the two newcomers had joined their comrade-in-arms in a heap on the lift platform. Gripping the Endorian's hand, Balzan led her down the steps to the roof level. The floor under them was trembling, moving gently up and down. Soon, it would be shaking as badly as the chamber far below; in a matter of minutes, as the tremors built through the foundations of the palace tower, the entire structure would come tumbling down . . . but that was *still* several minutes away. Time enough perhaps, Balzan reflected as he jerked Kitta along toward the gray wall of the arena, to do what he'd come here to do.

At least, he'd die trying.

The scene in the arena was like something out of a madhouse. Everywhere, men and women were struggling to push one another aside; Balzan saw one man punch an older woman across the back of the head, and climb over her unmoving form after she'd fallen to the ground. People screamed; several old men fainted. The arena was a cloud of dust as the tremors whipped up the sand in the battle area and sent it swirling around observers and combatants alike. The stench was almost overpowering: the stench of human fear, a stink composed of sweat, grime, the urine from fright-squeezed bladders, the vomit of the weaker citizens; and other, less wholesome odors. While Balzan stood at the top of the stairs, staring down at the churning mass of people, a new vibration shook the palace, evoking new screams and renewed effort. Balzan shook his head in disgust. A man hurried toward him, leading a pack of shrieking Kharnites. Balzan pushed Kitta back and let the mob pass; one of the women in the pack paused to grab his tunic and cry, "It's falling; the palace is falling," before rushing on, her conscience salved. At the exit leading from the arena into the palace proper—the direction in which the refugees from the Games were headed—a knot of tense guards stood with waiting spears, glancing at each other with obvious apprehension. The forward thrust of the mob was so great, the first dozen or so frontrunners found themselves pushed into the spears and impaled. Their expressions couldn't have shown more surprise and dismay than the soldiers', none of whom apparently understood what was going on.

The Games were already in progress, it seemed, when the tremors struck. In the arena itself, Balzan could see several huulats pacing around nervously, roaring among themselves as they eyed the group of petrified Endorians standing a short distance from the huulats on the arena

180

floor. Seeing the situation, he started shoving his way through the crowd clawing *up* the amphitheater stairs, going in a direction opposite to his own. Kitta followed behind, her hand clasped firmly in his.

The arena was immense, as large as the chamber in which the queen had held her final audience. This chamber, however, was open to the sky, a rather lowering sky at the moment, filled with black clouds and swept by far-off winds. The arena itself was set up in a semicircle, the spectator stands facing outward, overlooking the arena floor and, beyond that, the city. Not far from the floor, though separated from it by a high gate, was the docking port for the sky-ships. Several ships were berthed at the moment, and as Balzan made his way through the press of people toward the arena floor, he saw small figures scurrying around the immense ships, readying some for launching. He made a mental note of this and continued to force his way through the shouting, shrieking mob. At last, he broke from the crowd and stood on a relatively empty promenade above the arena floor. Kitta came up behind him.

"What are you going to do?" she cried.

"Help those people, if I can." He stripped off his tunic, leaving on only his tights, which were torn off at the mid-thigh. Gripping his sword, he vaulted over the railing and dropped the sixteen feet to the arena proper. His heart was beating quickly, and there was a roaring in his ears that came from a source other than the raging huulats; but he forced himself into a preternatural calm, and strode across the heaving sands toward the nearest huulat, who gazed at him with a mixture of nervousness, anger—and fear.

"Get to the far corner," Balzan called out to the Endorians, clotted together in a panicking group. "Don't move too quickly, or the huulats will attack you. But for god's sake, *move*." Under stress, he always turned to the epithets repeated to him by the Teacher when the computer was reading from the ship library of earth novels. The Endorians gaped at him, obviously not hearing him. He pointed with his free hand, made a gesture, and they got the idea. As they started to move, however, a particularly fierce tremor lifted the arena and shook it, throwing the Endorians to the ground. Balzan—who'd ridden the shock wave with relative ease—cursed as one massive huulat made a leap toward the Endorians, incited by the quake. Balzan also leaped, making contact with the huulat halfway.

Kitta had been right: the huulats of the arena *were* more ferocious than the Stalkers, more vicious and unpredictable. Sensing Balzan's attack, the huulat whirled and met him. The two closed. If he'd been fighting with anything but a neutron sword stolen from a palace guard, he wouldn't have had a chance; as it was, Balzan cut the creature in two with the first blow, then turned to perform a similar service for the others. One attacked; the other fled. Balzan bowed under the first huulat's head-high lunge, came around and swacked the creature with the flat end of his blade. The creature responded as Balzan expected, with a blind frontal attack that carried it down the full length of the human's sword before it realized it was dead. The huulat slipped off the sword, thumping heavily to the ground, and Balzan turned to face the remaining beast—only to find himself alone.

There was a commotion over near the stockade gate, the high bars which covered a passage leading directly from the yarrotite compound to the arena floor. Balzan checked out the Endorians, who'd followed his command and were cowering near the north wall, and then he raced across the sand—missing his step once when the ground wrenched, and a section of earth plummeted into a seemingly bottomless abyss. Arriving at the gate, he found Lio and Urro and a dozen other Kharnites fumbling with the lock from the inside. Naturally, the guards were long gone, and even if they hadn't been, no Kharnite soldier would consider releasing a prisoner, even if the palace *were* crumbling under him. Lio brightened when he saw Balzan; then he blanched, realizing that the young human should logically be long dead.

"I'll tell you later," Balzan said as he cut the lock free

with the glowing tip of his sword. "Are these all the yarrotites left?"

"Only the ones we could . . . ah . . . persuade, Balzan. The rest don't mind the idea of being crushed alive," Lio said sarcastically. "They're all so drugged, it's a wonder they remember to breathe."

"How'd you manage to unpoison so many?"

"Urro and I both took three at a time. After you killed Kalak, there was no trouble from the training staff; nobody cared if a few yarrotites were missing from practice . . . and we made sure they remained missing all day. Even missed their meals," he ended, smiling.

"Have them round up all the still-drugged yarrotites they can," Balzan said briskly, ignoring the joke. "*And* help the prisoners who were going to become huulat-meat. In case you haven't noticed, this tower has maybe two minutes left—after that, we'd better be long gone.

"I'm afraid you won't be going anywhere," said a voice.

Balzan spun around. Standing not ten feet away was Lord Sha, his whip unslung at his side, flanked by several dozen soldiers—all grim-looking, determined men. One of those grim-looking men was holding a struggling Kitta, gripping her around the waist and holding her a foot off the ground. Catching sight of Balzan, Kitta redoubled her efforts to smash the heel of her foot into the Kharnite's kneecap. Her captor just grinned.

"Don't be a fool," Balzan said to Sha. "The tower's collapsing. In a matter of moments it'll all be over. Don't throw away your life now."

"A slave does not give orders to Lord Sha," the lean Kharnite said, hissing. He grimaced as the tower shook violently beneath him. His guards reacted with varying degrees of concern, from clear terror on the face of the youngest soldier, to mindless apathy on the part of Kitta's soldier, who simply smiled more broadly and laughed as the Endorian squirmed in his thick-handed grasp.

"You're Sha?" Balzan asked slowly. Urro's one good eye swiveled to watch Balzan, the heavy-set bearded man's broad face taking on a look of interest.

"I am."

183

"Then you're the man I've come here to see."

"I?" Sha looked puzzled. After a moment, his face cleared. "I take it you are the queen's new lover?"

Balzan shook his head. "My friend, she's no use for lovers where she is now. She's dead."

Sha's scream of rage exploded at the same moment that a section of the tower wall snapped away, to go plummeting toward the city. He came at Balzan with his sword drawn, and the young human had time only to wrench his own sword up to meet Sha's blow. They parried, backed away from each other, closed again. Sha was muttering something unintelligible. His eyes were pinpricks of light—mad light—in a face chiseled from jade. He snorted as he fought, grunting with a combination of rage and physical exertion. Beneath the two swordsmen, the tower shuddered—and slowly began to come apart.

Urro said something to Lio, broke away from the knot of yarrotites, and plunged toward Balzan. Out of the corner of his eye, Balzan saw Urro approaching, tugging at something he carried under his tunic. The massive one-eyed man's hand came out, holding something. Balzan reacted with shock, almost missed one of Lord Sha's thrusts, and applied himself once more to a deft countering of the Kharnite's every blow. He felt a hand touch him briefly on the shoulder, felt something pressed into his own hand, and only then, breaking from Sha, did he look down.

It was his therb. Kalak had kept it with the weapons in the armory and hadn't allowed Balzan to use it, considering it too exotic for a trainee yarrotite. With Kalak dead, Urro must have simply stolen the weapon, knowing Balzan would want it, if and when he ever returned.

Well, thought Balzan, he had returned . . . and it was time he made use of Urro's gift.

Thinking that, he threw his sword at Sha, skipped back a few yards and unhooked his therb, shaking it out in one practiced motion.

Sha, seeing this, dropped his sword as well, and reached for his own whip.

The two men circled each other, then, at the outer limits

of their whips' effective range. Balzan tried a few practice flicks, sending the tip of the barb toward Sha's brow, letting it fall just a fraction of an inch short. Sha acted in a similar fashion, snapping his own barb tip within inches of Balzan's right hand. For a time, neither man moved. They remained motionless, and the yarrotites and the soldiers alike also remained motionless—while the tower continued to shake, throb—

Suddenly, a complete section of the tower sank from view. Part of the arena went with it, sending the Kharnites sprawling. Only Sha and Balzan retained their footing, since both men were trying their best to gain a steady balance. Balzan flicked his therb; the barbed tip, with its charge of poison, snapped beside Sha's ear. The Kharnite lord ducked, then sent his own whip cracking. Balzan jumped, and the whip cracked under him. Sha swung his whip back, was about to bring it forward again, when Balzan leaned toward the lord, and in a graceful, easy movement—cut his whip tip across Sha's throat, slicing a green line through the tight flesh. Sha's eyes bugged; he opened his mouth to cry out. Blood gushed up between his lips, spurted from his neck. His knees buckled and he fell, jerked once . . . and was finished.

3.

"This way."

The others didn't question; they followed. There'd been a brief—extremely brief—battle with the soldiers who'd remained faithful to Sha after his death, and as a result of that battle any of the yarrotites who might have spurned Balzan's authority before, doubted it no longer. In a group they ran, gathering up survivors as they went, organizing the Endorians and the other captives who'd been destined to die in the arena. It was a small band, in proportion to the number of people who'd been brought to the city for the Games, but even so there were almost a hundred men and women following Balzan when he hurried through the north gate of the arena, toward the tethered sky-ships. A hundred survivors . . . out of how many thousands who'd died in that amphitheater, to feed Myrane's ambitions? Balzan tried not to think about those lost dead; he concentrated on the present. Only the present could count.

They arrived on the docking platform and forced their way past the hysterical guards. There was little resistance; the soldiers had remained at their posts because they were too frightened to do anything else, too paralyzed with fear and too stupid to make their own decisions. Most of the sky-ships were gone, launched by their crews and their masters into the swirling storm clouds, in an effort to avoid the fate overtaking the towering palace of Kharn. Only the *Starskimmer* and one other ship remained. Balzan sent half the escaped prisoners to the second ship, took the first ship for his own, overseeing the loading of the Endorians, coaxing them, urging them, commanding them when all else failed. Many of the Endorians didn't want to leave; they couldn't understand that they'd been freed. Finally, frustrated by the time these arguments were taking, Balzan developed a simple reply to any Endorian protesting the escape: the sharp application of the flat of his sword. The reply was admirably received.

Only moments after the prisoners had swarmed over the dock, the sky-ships cast free. There was no thought of attaching reins and harnesses to the gaapurs kept in the stables below; there was no time for such niceties. The restraining ropes were cut. The ships drifted away, the docking platform swinging off to the right and down as the ships caught a thermal updraft and swept toward the clouds. From vantage points along the railings of the two ships, the prisoners watched the last moments of the palace, and some of the prisoners, a few, found themselves wondering about those remaining in the tower . . . those who didn't escape . . .

Those about to die.

4.

In his chamber, the Red Lord listened to the sounds of death and dying, and a smile crossed his withered lips.

His slave, seated at his master's feet, saw the smile and paled, horrified.

"It's our end, my lord," the slave cried. "The end of Kharn! How can you smile?"

Dragus opened his mouth to answer, to give a reason that would have been meaningless to the youthful slave, but before he could speak, a beam from the ceiling plummeted downward, thrusting through him and pinning him to the floor like a squashed fly.

The slave died a moment later, screaming as the floor gave way around him and he fell to a distant doom.

On his way down a ramp leading from the arena to the lift capsules, in the midst of a crowd of men and women heading toward the same goal, Yurl, the palace surgeon, felt someone step on the rear of his heavy physician's cloak. The clasp around his throat snapped taut against his windpipe. He tripped, fell to the ground, choking and grappling to release the clasp before the tangled cloak strangled him.

Within ten seconds, he was trampled to a bloody pulp.

As Gamemaster, he should have known a hundred secret exits from the arena, but Trito had always been more concerned with the pleasures of his position, as opposed to the less enjoyable "duties."

He was still searching for a way out of his private box —the regular exit being blocked by a collapsed wall— when the section of the palace tower containing the arena abruptly crumbled in on itself.

He was caught between two sliding walls as he fell. For a moment he remained alive, suspended. Then the walls slammed together, grinding into a powder, and Trito, like all the rest, passed from the world.

The destruction lasted almost an hour. Wall caved in on wall, level collapsed onto level, the whole tower dropping in on itself like a castle of sand. The watchers in the sky-ships remained at their posts for the full hour, their eyes aching after a time, their backs complaining wearily of the strain. Mesmerized by the weird beauty of the fall, they were unable to look away. Only Balzan turned his back on the scene of carnage. Only Balzan felt a wave of pity, and sadness, and even regret, when the last bit of dust cleared, and the last stone toppled slowly over. . . .

When it was done, he went below. Kitta found him in the main saloon a few minutes after he entered. She looked at him from the doorway, and something in his posture warned her he wanted privacy. Timidly, she left.

He listened to her go.

Epilogue

Ten days after leaving the city of Kharn, the *Starskimmer,* drifting, touched down on the peak of a mountain in a range far to the northwest of that land. Harsh winds whipped the peak, and there was snow down to the timberline, but even so, Balzan made clear his intention to leave. Lio offered to go with him, but the young human refused.

"I've learned something about myself, Lio. I'm not like you, not like the others. I'm different inside, as well as outside. I feel things you don't; I see things you can't see. Until I understand myself fully, I'll never be able to deal with you, or the others, or the world, the way I should." He drew a breath of the cold air, let it out in a frosty cloud. "I asked a friend once, what is a man? I can tell you this: a man *feels*. He feels more strongly than an Endorian, because he cares for *ideas* as well as people. And he feels more strongly than a Kharnite, because he cares even for his enemies. I saw you with the others, watching those people die, that tower fall. . . ." Balzan shuddered, from the cold, and from the memory. "That wasn't something I could enjoy. They deserved it, yes, but I couldn't enjoy *watching* it happen."

He broke off, looked around at Lio, who stood beside him at the railing of the sky-ship, a few yards above the snow-covered mountainside. Balzan was dressed warmly, though sparingly, in furs they'd found in the storage cabin. At his side, he carried his therb; he'd left the neutron sword on the dock in Kharn. Lio wore fewer furs; his reptilian body adapted to temperature changes easily, even to such intense cold.

"You're certain you want it this way?" the Kharnite asked.

"Absolutely."

Lio shrugged and held out his hand. Balzan grasped it. "I hope I meet you again somewhere," Lio said. "I'd like to think we're friends."

"We are, Lio. We are."

Gripping the metal railing, wincing at the bitter cold that struck at him even through heavy gloves, Balzan swung up and leaped the distance to the mountainside. The ship bobbed as he left it; regaining his balance, Balzan turned to watch it rise once more into the pale green sky. He caught a glimpse of a figure on the main deck, a slim figure bundled in furs, her head uncovered, her fur ruffled by the wind. He raised a hand and waved. Kitta lifted her own hand, moved it once, then hurried out of sight.

The *Starskimmer* rose, and slowly, reluctantly, dwindled from view.

Balzan watched it go; eventually, he turned and started down toward the distant green land below.

are you missing out on some great Pyramid books?

You can have any title in print at Pyramid delivered right to your door! To receive your Pyramid Paperback Catalog, fill in the label below (use a ball point pen please) and mail to Pyramid . . .

PYRAMID PUBLICATIONS
Mail Order Department
9 Garden Street
Moonachie, New Jersey 07074

NAME_____.

ADDRESS_____

CITY_____STATE_____

P-5   ZIP_____